"What I want, Sebastian, is for you to tell me the truth."

He glanced up at her, his face annoyingly bland. "About what?"

"About everything."

"Everything."

"You know what I mean, so don't play dumb. It doesn't suit you."

"What if I think you're not ready to know...everything?"

Miranda Lee

AUNT LUCY'S LOVER

Passion™

HARLEQUIN®

TORONTO • NEW YORK • LONDON
AMSTERDAM • PARIS • SYDNEY • HAMBURG
STOCKHOLM • ATHENS • TOKYO • MILAN • MADRID
PRAGUE • WARSAW • BUDAPEST • AUCKLAND

ISBN 0-373-12099-0

AUNT LUCY'S LOVER

First North American Publication 2000.

Copyright © 1996 by Miranda Lee.

Visit us at www.romance.net

Printed in U.S.A.

CHAPTER ONE

'YOUR Aunt Lucy has left you everything.'

Jessica stared at the solicitor across his leather-topped desk. 'Everything?' she repeated blankly, her normally sharp brain a little fuzzy with shock.

She was still getting over the news of Aunt Lucy's death. Of inoperable cancer, three weeks earlier.

When she'd protested over not being told at the time, the solicitor informed her this was because no one had known of her existence till her aunt's will had been found a couple of days ago.

Jessica had not known of her Aunt Lucy's existence, either, till the woman herself had shown up at the Sydney Grand a couple of months back and asked to speak to the hotel's public relations manager, who was none other than Jessica herself.

It had been an awkward meeting. Jessica had been stunned when the woman abruptly announced she was her mother's older sister. Jessica's mother had always claimed she was a foundling, with no known relatives.

Aunt Lucy had seemed a little stunned herself by the sight of her niece. She'd stared and stared at her, as though she'd been confronted by a ghost. When Jessica was called away to a problem with one of the guests, she'd left the tongue-tied woman in her office with the promise to return shortly. There were so many questions

Jessica had wanted to ask. My God, her head had been whirling with them.

But when she'd returned fifteen minutes later, her Aunt Lucy had disappeared.

The memory of the woman's distressed face had tormented Jessica ever since. As had the many questions her aunt's brief and mysterious visit had caused. Why had her mother lied to her? Why hadn't her aunt waited for her to come back? And why had she stared at her so strangely, as though her physical appearance offended her?

Jessica had tried tracing her aunt, but without success. She'd almost got to the stage where she was prepared to hire a private investigator. Only this last week, she'd started searching for one in the yellow pages.

As sad as her Aunt Lucy's death was, at least now she might find some answers to her many questions. To which was added the puzzle of why her aunt had made her—a niece she'd only met once—her one and only heir!

'I can see you're startled by this legacy, Miss Rawlins,' the solicitor said. 'But Mrs. Hardcourt's will is quite clear.'

'*Mrs*. Hardcourt?' Jessica immediately picked up on the title. 'My aunt was married, then?'

No wonder she hadn't been able to trace her. She'd tried Woods, which had been her mother's maiden name.

'She was a widow. For some considerable years, I gather. She had no children of her own. Your mother was her only sibling. Their parents passed away many years back.'

Jessica's heart sank. There went her hope of grandparents, or other aunts and uncles, or even cousins. So she still had no living family who wanted anything to do with her. Her own father—plus his parents and relatives—had abandoned all contact after her mother divorced him.

Not that Jessica had ever really known them. She'd only been three at the time of her parents' divorce, and it had been a bitter parting, one her mother refused to speak of afterwards.

When Jessica had notified her father by telephone of her mother's death eight years ago—he still lived in Sydney—he hadn't even had the decency to attend the funeral.

Jessica's heart turned over as she thought of that wretched day. It had been raining, with no one at the graveside except herself, the priest and the undertakers. Her mother had had no close friends, having been an agoraphobic and an alcoholic for as long as Jessica could remember. She'd died, of liver and kidney failure, at the age of thirty-eight.

Jessica wondered anew what had been behind her mother's self-loathing and misery. She'd thought it was her failed marriage. Now she wasn't so sure.

So many questions about her mother's and her own life, unanswered...

Jessica looked up at the patiently waiting solicitor, her expression curious and thoughtful.

'Surely my aunt's husband must have had some relatives,' she speculated. 'Why didn't she leave them something? Why leave everything to me?'

The solicitor shrugged. 'I'm afraid I don't know the answer to that. She doesn't mention any in-laws in her will. Neither have any come forward. You are her sole legal heir, and might I say her estate is quite considerable.'

Jessica was taken aback. She'd been picturing a small

house perhaps, in a country town. Somehow, Aunt Lucy had looked country. Jessica hadn't envisaged any great fortune. 'How considerable is considerable?' she asked, feeling the first stirring of excitement.

One of Jessica's primary goals in life had been to make herself financially secure. Being poor all her young life had left its mark. When little more than a child, she had vowed never to be poor once she was old enough to support herself. After her mother's death, she'd worked damned hard to put herself into a position where she had a well-paid job with considerable job security.

Though no job was entirely secure in this day and age, she conceded.

'Firstly, there is the property,' the solicitor began enthusiastically. 'It consists of several acres of prime real estate overlooking the Pacific, and a grand old heritage home, which your aunt had been running as a guesthouse for many years. There is no mortgage, and the house itself is reputedly well-furnished with solid pieces, many of them valuable antiques.'

'Goodness!' Jessica exclaimed. 'I had no idea!'

'So I can see. I am also pleased to inform you that even after all legal fees and funeral expenses are paid for, your aunt's bank balance will still be slightly in excess of five hundred thousand dollars.'

Jessica gasped. 'Half a million dollars!' She could hardly believe her ears. 'So where *is* this property? You mentioned an acreage. And a view of the Pacific Ocean. I presume it's along the east coast somewhere, then?'

The solicitor looked surprised. 'You mean you don't know where your aunt lived?'

'No, I told you. I hardly knew her. We only met the once.'

'I see. You're in for another surprise then. Your Aunt Lucy lived on Norfolk Island.'

'Norfolk Island!'

'Yes.'

'Good Lord.' Jessica had never been to Norfolk Island, but she knew where it was. Out in the Pacific Ocean off the east coast of Australia. It was a popular holiday destination for honeymooners and the middle-aged to elderly, the sort of pretty but peaceful place where the most exciting activity available was looking through the ruins of an old convict gaol. One of the staff at the hotel had spent a week there last year and left a tourist brochure lying around. Jessica recalled glancing at it and thinking she'd be bored to tears at a place like that.

Jessica liked to keep busy. And she liked lots of people around her; another mark, perhaps, of her wretched childhood when she'd had no friends, as well as no money. You didn't bring friends home to a drunken mother, and if you had no money, you couldn't afford to go out.

The inner Sydney area was Jessica's type of place. She thrived on the hustle and bustle of city life, the bright lights and the continuous undercurrent of throbbing life. When she wasn't working, there was always some place to go, something to do. Dining out and discos. The theatre. The ballet. Movies. Concerts.

Jessica couldn't imagine living anywhere else, certainly not on a small Pacific island whose only bright lights were the stars in the sky!

'I presume you'd like to go and see your inheritance for yourself?' the solicitor asked.

Jessica gnawed at her bottom lip. Well, of course she would. But she really didn't have the time right now. Her job was very demanding, and February was still a busy month for hotels in Sydney.

Still, how could she pass up the opportunity to find out the truth about her roots? And where better to start than where her aunt lived? It was clear the solicitor didn't know very much.

Jessica mulled over her work situation. She *was* due her annual holidays, having slaved for over a year in her present position without a break. Surely they could spare her for a week or two. She would demand compassionate leave if the boss made a fuss.

'Yes, I *would* like to see it,' she said, making up her mind with her usual decisiveness. 'I should be able to arrange to have the property put up for sale while I'm there, too, shouldn't I?'

The solicitor seemed startled. 'You mean you don't want to live there yourself?'

'Heavens, no. My life is here, in Sydney.'

'You do realise that people with permanent residency on Norfolk Island don't pay any income tax,' he said dryly.

Jessica had forgotten about that. It was a tempting thought—especially now, with her income about to soar—but such a consideration was still not enough for her to give up a career she'd slaved for and a lifestyle she enjoyed. What on earth would she do on Norfolk Island?

'You could take over the running of your aunt's guesthouse,' the solicitor said, as though reading her mind. 'You'd have no trouble securing a permit to stay under your circumstances.'

Jessica wrinkled her nose. She'd spent a year in hotel housekeeping while working her way up in her career, and had hated it. She knew exactly what running a guesthouse would entail, and it was not what she wanted to do with her life.

'That's not for me, I'm afraid. No, I'll be selling up and investing the money.'

'I see. Er, how long were you planning on staying on the island?'

'A fortnight at the most,' Jessica said crisply. 'I can't spare more time than that.'

'Hm, I think you'll have to, Miss Rawlins. You see, there is a small but rather odd condition attached to your inheriting your aunt's estate.'

'Really? You didn't mention anything earlier.'

'I was presuming you'd want to live there permanently. Most people would jump at the chance. Since you don't, then within a reasonable time of your being notified of your aunt's death, you have to take up residence in her home on the island and live there for at least one month.'

'A month! But that's ridiculous. I can't afford a month!'

'I'm afraid you'll have to, if you wish to inherit. Your aunt's wishes are clear. Provisions have even been made in the will to pay for the purchase of your airline ticket, in case you couldn't afford one. Oh, and there's another small condition. During this month, you are to allow a certain Mr. Slade to remain living in the same room he has occupied for the last three years, free of charge.'

'How very peculiar! What happens if I don't comply?'

'Then the estate goes to the aforementioned Mr. Slade, whom Mrs. Hardcourt describes in her will as having been a loyal and loving companion to her over these past three years.'

Jessica frowned. Was loyal and loving companion a euphemism for lover? She remembered her aunt as having been a handsome woman, with a good figure for her age. Although obviously in her fifties, it was not inconceivable she'd been having an intimate physical relationship with a man.

'It was this Mr. Slade who found the will,' the solicitor said. 'It had apparently slipped down behind a drawer. He's been living in and looking after the house and grounds since your aunt's death.'

'Not to mention searching for a will, which he obviously knew existed,' Jessica pointed out dryly. For some reason, she didn't like the sound of this Mr. Slade. Or was it just the complication of that odd condition she didn't like? 'I wonder why my aunt didn't just leave everything to him in the first place, if they were so close?'

'I really couldn't say.'

'No, of course not,' Jessica murmured. The only way she was going to find out anything was to go there herself. But for a whole month? How was she going to wangle that without risking her job?

'This Mr. Slade,' she said, her mind ticking over. 'What do you know about him?'

'Very little. I did speak to him briefly on the telephone yesterday.'

'And?'

'He sounded surprisingly...young.'

'*Young?*' Jessica repeated, startled.

'It was just an impression. Some quite elderly people have young-sounding telephone voices.'

Jessica nodded. That was so true. The owner of the Sydney Grand was well into his sixties but sounded much younger on the telephone.

'There's a flight leaving for Norfolk Island next Sunday morning at seven,' the solicitor informed her. 'If you like, I can call the airline right now and see if they have a spare seat. If you go now, you'll only have to stay four weeks to satisfy your aunt's will. February this year only has twenty-eight days.'

So it had. But four weeks away from the hotel at this time of the year? Her boss would be most put out. Still, what alternative did she have?

'All right,' Jessica agreed.

Now that her mind was made up, she was quite eager to be on her way, her female curiosity more than a little piqued. She wanted to see the place for herself. And the island. And the mysterious Mr. Slade.

Actually, she felt a bit guilty about him. If he'd genuinely loved her aunt and nursed her during her last days, surely he deserved more for his devotion than one month's free board. Jessica decided that if he proved to have been a genuine friend to her aunt and was in any way hard up for money, she would give him a cash legacy. It was the least she could do.

'Would you like the telephone number of your aunt's house?' the solicitor asked once his call to the airline had been successfully completed. 'That way you can call this Mr. Slade yourself and arrange for him to pick you up at the airport when you arrive.'

'All right,' Jessica agreed again. It would be interesting to see how young he sounded to *her*. Maybe the solicitor thought fifty was young. He was nearing sixty himself.

He jotted down her aunt's number on the back of one of his business cards and handed it over to Jessica, who slipped it into her handbag.

'Don't hesitate to call me if you need any help,' he said, standing up when she did so.

Jessica shook his extended hand. 'Thank you,' she said. 'I will.'

As she turned and walked out of the office, the sudden

thought came that her life was never going to be the same
again. Suddenly, she was a rich woman, an heiress.

Strange. The realisation was vaguely unsettling.
Jessica decided then and there not to tell anyone at work,
or even any of her friends. Aside from the jealousy it
might inspire, people treated you differently when you
were rich, especially the opposite sex.

Of course, there were a couple of people who already
knew of her new financial status. That couldn't be
helped. But the solicitor was hardly going to present a
problem in her day-to-day life. He wasn't likely to make
a play for her, either.

Which left only Mr. Slade.

Jessica almost laughed at the instant tightening in her
stomach. Now she was being fanciful. Logically, Mr.
Slade had to at least be in his fifties. Neither was he
likely to be too enamoured with the woman who'd
robbed him of a sizeable inheritance. He might very well
resent her.

Suddenly, the month she had to spend on Norfolk
Island in the same house as Mr. Slade loomed as very
awkward, indeed.

Well, that was just too bad, Jessica thought fatalisti-
cally. She had every right to go there, and every right to
find out what she could about her own and her mother's
past!

CHAPTER TWO

JESSICA'S watch said nine-thirty as she unlocked the front door of her flat. Her sigh was a little weary as she stepped inside and switched on the lights. She'd stayed extra late at the hotel tonight, getting things organised so that her PA could manage without her for the next month.

In the end, she'd asked for her full four weeks' holidays, saying she was suffering from emotional stress after the sudden death of a dear aunt. The hotel management hadn't been thrilled with the short notice, but they hadn't been as difficult about her request as she'd imagined they'd be. Clearly, they valued her as an employee and didn't want to lose her.

Jessica was well aware she did a good job, but it had always faintly worried her that she'd won her present position more for her model-like looks than her qualifications. Not that she didn't have plenty of those, as well. A degree in hotel management and tourism, plus years of experience working in every facet of the hotel industry from housekeeping to reception to guest relations.

Jessica closed the door of her near-new North Sydney apartment—an airy two-bedroomed unit with a lovely view of the bridge and harbour. She'd bought it only four months previously, the deposit alone taking every cent she had saved during her working life.

But she'd craved her own place after sharing rented accommodation for years.

Funnily enough, whilst she adored the bathroom and bedroom privacy, she wasn't finding living alone quite as satisfying a way of life as she'd thought it would be. She missed not having anyone to talk to in the evenings. Lately, she'd felt awfully lonely, which was unfortunate. In the past, whenever her chronic loneliness reached these depths, she had launched into an affair with some highly unsuitable man.

Of course she never knew they were unsuitable at the time, since they always declared their undying love and devotion at first, to which she invariably responded.

It was only later, when she found out they were married, or an addict of some sort, or allergic to long-term commitment, that she recognised her own folly for what it was. Just desperation to feel loved and not be alone, and a deep desire to find the man of her dreams, marry him and have so many children she would never be alone again!

At that point the scales would fall from her eyes and she would see her great love for what he was—usually no more than a handsome and highly accomplished liar who was using her for what he could get and giving her very little in return, not even good sex!

Jessica knew from talking to girlfriends and reading women's magazines that she had always been short-changed in the bedroom department. Perhaps she should have complained at the time, but you just didn't when you imagined you were madly in love.

The thought of going that road again made her shudder. Better she remain alone than involved with one of those. Better she remain unmarried and childless than shackled to some selfish guy who would make a lousy father and who didn't even satisfy her in bed!

Which left *what* to cure her present loneliness?

'A flatmate!' she decided aloud. 'A female, of course,' she added dryly as she strode down the small hallway and into her bedroom, tossing her handbag onto the double bed and kicking off her shoes.

'Stuff men!' she muttered as she began to strip.

One particular man suddenly jumped into her mind.

Her Aunt Lucy's lover—the enigmatic Mr. Slade. She'd been going to ring him earlier at the office, but had kept putting it off. It irked her that she felt nervous about ringing him.

Ring him now, her pride demanded. *What's wrong with you? So he might give you the cold shoulder—you can't help that. Just be polite, anyway. You're used to being polite to some of the rudest and most arrogant men around. Your job has trained you for it. Use some of that training now!*

Jessica glared over at the telephone, which sat on the bedside table nearest the window. Lifting her chin, she moved over to snatch up her handbag from the bed, opened it and drew out the business card the solicitor had given her. She didn't delay once the number was in her hands. She sat down and dialled straight away before she procrastinated further.

'Hi there,' said a male voice at last. 'Seb here.'

Jessica frowned. If 'Seb here' was Mr. Slade, then he did indeed sound young. Far too young to be the lover of a woman in her fifties. Unless...

Her stomach contracted at the thought her aunt might have fallen into the clutches of the type of unconscionable young man who preyed on wealthy widows. Jessica was not unfamiliar with the species. They often hung around the bars in the hotel, waiting and watching for suitable prey. They were invariably handsome. And charming. And young.

If Mr. Slade turned out to be one of those, she thought crossly, he would get short shrift after the month was over. He would not get a cent from her. Not one single cent!

'This is Jessica Rawlins,' she said, simmering outrage giving her voice a sharp edge. 'Would I be speaking to Mr. Slade?'

'You sure are. Pleased to hear from you, Jessica. I presume Lucy's solicitor has been in touch. So when are you coming over?'

Jessica's eyebrows lifted. Well, he was certainly straight to the point, and not at all resentful sounding. If she hadn't been on her toes, she might have been totally disarmed by his casual charm.

'I'm catching the seven o'clock flight from Sydney on Sunday,' she said stiffly.

'I'll meet you then. Oops, no, I can't. I promised Mike I'd go fishing with him Sunday morning. Tell you what, I'll get Evie to meet you.'

'And who, pray tell, is Evie?' she asked archly.

'Evie? She was your aunt's chief cook and bottle washer. You'll like Evie,' he went on blithely. 'Everyone does. Now perhaps you'd better tell me what you look like, so she won't have any trouble recognising you on Sunday. Are you tall?'

'Reasonably,' Jessica bit out after smothering her frustration. She supposed she'd find out everything she wanted to know soon enough. And she could trust her eyes far more than a conversation on the telephone.

'Slim?' he went on.

'Yes.'

'What colour hair?'

'Black.'

'Long or short?'

'Shoulder-length, but I always wear it up.'

'How old are you? Approximately,' he added quickly with humour in his voice.

'Twenty-eight,' Jessica said, having no reason to hide her age.

'Really. You *sound* older.'

She tried not to take offence, and failed. 'Well, you don't,' she snapped.

'I don't what?'

'Sound as old as I thought you'd be. If I didn't know better, I'd say you were no more than thirty.'

His laughter might have been infectious under other circumstances. 'You've no idea how many people say that to me, Jessica,' he said. 'But it's some years since I saw thirty.'

Jessica wasn't sure if she was mollified by that statement or not. She should have been relieved to find he was respectably middle-aged, but she didn't feel relieved. She felt decidedly nettled. Mr. Slade was rubbing her the wrong way, for some reason.

'I *look* young for my age, too,' he volunteered. 'But I try not to worry about it.'

She could hear the smile in his voice and bristled some more.

'By the way, bring your swimmers and shorts with you,' he added. 'It's pretty warm here at the moment. How long will you be staying?'

'Just the month.'

'Ah,' he said with a long sigh. 'What a pity. Still, we can talk about that more when you get here. I'm glad you rang, Jessica. I'm really looking forward to meeting you. I'm just sorry I can't welcome you myself at the airport. I'll try to get back by the time you arrive at the house. Au revoir for now. Have a good flight.'

He hung up, leaving Jessica not sure what she thought about him now. Clearly, he *was* middle-aged. He'd been most amused at her saying he sounded thirty.

If she were honest, she had to admit he'd been very nice to her, and not at all resentful of her inheritance. She wondered what he wanted to talk to her about. Did he hope to persuade her to stay and run the guesthouse? If he did, then he'd be wasting his breath. She had no intention of doing any such thing.

But she did want to talk to *him*. She wanted to find out everything he knew about her aunt. Maybe this Evie would know things, as well, depending on how many years she'd been Aunt Lucy's cook.

Thinking of cooks reminded Jessica how hungry she was. Levering herself up from the bed, she headed for the door and the kitchen, dressed in nothing but her camisole and pantihose. She caught a glimpse of herself in the mirrored wardrobe as she passed and recalled the rather bland details she'd given Mr. Slade. Twenty-eight, tall, slim, black hair, worn up.

Not much of a description. Difficult to form a complete picture. But she could hardly have added she had a face that wouldn't have looked out of place on the cover of *Vogue*, and a body one of her lovers had said he'd kill for.

He had certainly *lied* for it, she thought tartly.

'And what do *you* look like, Mr. Slade?' she mused out loud as she continued on to the kitchen. 'Tall, I'll bet. And slim. Men who look young for their age are always slim. And you won't be bald. No way. You'll have a full head of hair with only a little grey. And you'll be handsome, won't you, Mr. Slade? In a middle-aged sort of way. And just a little bit of a ladies' man, I'll warrant.'

Jessica wondered anew if he'd really been her aunt's lover, or just a good friend. He'd said nothing to indicate either way. Really, she hadn't handled that call very well. She'd found out absolutely nothing! Mr. Slade's youthful voice and manner had sent her off on a cynical tangent, and by the time she'd realised her mistake, the call had been over.

Still, it was only three days till Sunday. Not long. In no time she'd be landing at Norfolk Island airport and be right on the doorstep of discovering all she wanted to know.

A nervous wave rippled down Jessica's spine, and she shivered. It had not escaped her logical mind that something pretty awful must have happened for her mother to lie like she had. Maybe she'd done something wicked and shameful, then run away from home. Or something wicked and shameful had been done to *her*, with the same result.

Jessica wasn't sure what that something could have been. Whatever had happened, she meant to find out the truth. Oh, yes, she meant to find out everything!

CHAPTER THREE

JESSICA'S flight on Sunday morning took two and a half hours. Two and a half long hours of butterflies in her stomach. Some due to her fear of flying; most to fear of the unknown that awaited her on Norfolk Island.

She stared through her window the whole way, despite high cloud preventing a view of the ocean below. Not that she was really looking. She was thinking, and speculating, and worrying. It was only when they began their descent that the sight of the island itself jolted her back to the physical reality of her destination.

Goodness, but it *was* picturesque, a dot of deep tropical green within a wide blue expanse of sea. But so *small*! Jessica knew from the travel brochures that the island only measured five kilometres by eight. This hadn't bothered her till she saw that the airstrip was even smaller. She hoped the plane could stop in time, that it wouldn't plunge off the end of the runway into the sea.

The plane began to bank steeply at that moment, a wing blocking Jessica's view of the island. All she could see was water—deep, deep water. Her insides started to churn. She did so hate flying, especially the landing part.

The plane landed without incident, thank heavens, quickly taxiing over to a collection of small terminal buildings. There was a short delay while everything was sprayed for God knows what and some lady with a foreign accent gave a brief talk over the intercom about the island and its rules and regulations.

Jessica rolled her eyes when she heard the speed limit was only fifty kilometres an hour around the island generally, and a crawling twenty-five kilometres an hour through the town and down on the foreshores at Kingston. Drivers were warned they had to give way to all livestock on the roads.

Lord, she thought with rueful amusement. This was as far removed from Sydney as one could get!

The formalities finally over, she hoisted her roomy tan handbag onto her shoulder and alighted, relieved to find that it wasn't all that hot outside, despite the sun beginning to peep through the parting clouds. She'd worn a summer-weight pants-suit for travelling, a tailored cream outfit that didn't crease. But it had a lined jacket and wasn't the coolest thing she owned.

Her hair was cool, though, slicked back into the tight chic knot she always wore for work. Her makeup was expertly done to highlight her big dark eyes and full mouth. Her jewellery was discreet and expensive. A gold chain around her neck. Gold studs in her lobes. A gold watch around her slender wrist.

She looked sleek and sophisticated, and a lot more composed than she was feeling.

The short walk across the tarmac to the small customs building was enough for Jessica to see that whilst the air temperature felt moderate, the humidity was high. As soon as she arrived at her aunt's house she'd change into something lighter.

In no time Jessica had secured her suitcase and was through customs. It seemed there *was* some advantage coming to tiny places like this. She'd barely walked into the terminal building when a funny little barrel-shaped woman with frizzy grey hair touched her on the arm.

'You'd have to be Jessica,' she said, smiling up at her.

'And you must be Evie,' Jessica responded, smiling back. Impossible not to. Mr. Slade had been right about that. Evie was the sort of person one liked on sight. She had a round face with twinkling grey eyes and a warm smile. She wore a shapeless floral tent dress and might have been sixty.

Jessica was given a brief but all-encompassing appraisal. 'You don't look much like your mother, do you?'

She certainly didn't. Her mother had been petite and fair with blue eyes.

Still, Jessica's heart leapt at Evie's observation.

'You *knew* my mother?'

'Well, of course I knew your mother, lovie! I've lived on this island for near nigh forty years now. Everyone knows everyone around here. You'll soon learn that. I knew your grandparents, too. Come on,' Evie urged, taking her arm. 'Let's get out of this crowd and into some fresh air.'

Jessica allowed herself to be led down some steps and out into a half-empty car park. Her thoughts were whirling. If Evie had known her grandparents, did that mean they'd lived here on this island, as well? Had her aunt and her mother been *born* here? Were her family *islanders*?

The desire to bombard Evie with questions was great, but something held Jessica back for the moment. Probably an instinctive reluctance to admit she was so ignorant about her own past.

Or was she afraid to find out the truth, now that it was within her grasp?

'The car's over here,' Evie said.

It was a Mazda. Small, white, dented and dusty. It was also unlocked, with the keys in the ignition.

Jessica could not believe her eyes. 'Er, don't you think you should have locked your car?' she said as she climbed into the passenger seat, not wanting to criticise but unable to keep silent.

Evie laughed. 'No one locks their car on Norfolk Island, lovie. You'll get used to it.'

'I doubt it,' Jessica muttered, shaking her head. Imagine doing such a silly thing in Sydney!

'Think about it,' Evie said, starting up the engine. 'Where are they going to go if they steal it?'

Jessica had to admit that was true, but she knew she'd still be locking the car doors, no matter what the locals did.

'It's not my car, actually,' Evie added as she angled her way out of the car park. 'It used to belong to Lucy, but she gave it to Sebastian before she died.'

Jessica frowned at this news. So Mr. Slade *had* been given something, after all. Okay, so it wasn't much of a car but maybe he'd been given other gifts, as well. For all she knew, her aunt might have handed over quite a degree of money to her loyal and loving companion before she died. It would explain why he'd received nothing in the will.

'This is the main street,' Evie piped up. 'A lot of the shops have duty-free goods, you know. It's one of the main pastimes for visitors. Shopping.'

There were, indeed, a lot of shops lining the road. Some of them were open but most looked pretty well deserted, as were the sidewalks. There was a young boy on a bike, plus a middle-aged couple wandering along, hand in hand. It looked as quiet and dead a place as Jessica had originally thought.

'It's pretty slow on a Sunday,' Evie said. 'Things will be hopping here tomorrow.'

Jessica decided Evie's idea of hopping might be a fraction different from her own.

'Sebastian seemed to think you might want me to come in and do the shopping and cooking while you're here, like I did for Lucy,' Evie rattled on. 'He's been looking after himself and the place since Lucy's death, though I do drop by occasionally to give the house a dust through. I only live next door and men never think of dusting.'

'That was kind of you, Evie. Yes, I think I would like you to do that. I'll pay you whatever Lucy did. Will that be all right?'

Evie waved her indifference to talking about payment. 'Whatever. I don't really need the money,' she said. 'My husband left me plenty when he died. I just like to keep busy. And I love cooking. Eating, too.' She grinned over at Jessica. 'So what do you like to eat? Do you have any favourite foods or dishes?'

'Not really. I'm not fussy at all. Cook whatever you like. I'll just enjoy being pampered for a change. Cooking is not one of my strong points.'

Actually, she could cook quite well, had had to when she was growing up to survive. If she'd waited for her mother to cook her a meal she would have starved. But she didn't fancy cooking for Mr. Slade. It had also crossed her mind that she'd be able to question Evie with more ease if she was around the house on a regular basis.

'That's fixed, then,' Evie said happily. 'I'll come in every morning around eleven-thirty and make lunch. Then I'll come back around five to cook dinner for seven-thirty. I don't do breakfast. Lucy always did that for herself. How does that sound?'

'Marvellous.' Jessica sighed her satisfaction with the arrangement and settled back to look around some more.

The wide streets of the shopping centre were quickly left behind and they moved onto a narrower road, with what looked like farms on either side. A few cows grazed lethargically along the common. The Mazda squeezed past a truck going the other way, then a car, then a utility, Jessica noting that Evie exchanged waves with all three drivers as they passed by.

She commented on this and was told it was a local custom, and that even the tourists got into the spirit of the Norfolk Island wave within a day of arrival. Jessica was quietly impressed with their friendliness, despite cynically thinking that if all Sydney drivers did that in city traffic, everyone would go barmy. Still, it was rather sweet, in a way.

'Here we are,' Evie announced, slowing down and turning into a gateway that had a cattle grid between its posts and an iron archway above, which said with proud simplicity, Lucy's Place.

The gravel driveway rose gradually, any view either side blocked with thickly wooded Norfolk pines. Finally, the pine borders ceased, and there in front of Jessica was the most beautiful old wooden house she had ever seen. Painted cream, with a green pitched iron roof and huge wooden verandas all round, it stood on the crest of the hill with a stately grandeur and dignity that were quite breathtaking.

Jessica was surprised, both by its elegant beauty and its effect on her. She'd heard of falling in love at first sight, but she'd always thought of that in connection with a man, not a house.

A sudden movement on the veranda snapped her out of her astonished admiration. Someone had been sitting there and was now standing up and moving towards the front steps. A man, dressed in shorts and nothing else, holding a tall glass in his hand. A young man with shoulder-length fair hair.

He stopped and leant against one of the posts at the top of the steps and watched as Evie brought the car round to a halt at the base of the front steps.

Jessica frowned at him through the passenger window. This couldn't be Mr. Slade, surely. She couldn't see the details of his face—it was in shadow—but that was not the body of a middle-aged man. Or the hair.

Maybe he was a workman. A gardener, perhaps. Or the man who mowed the lawns. There were plenty to mow, she'd noted, the house set in huge rolling lawns. There was quite a bit of garden, as well, beds of flowers underneath the verandas, backed by multicoloured hibiscus bushes.

'I see Sebastian made it back from fishing in time to greet you,' Evie said, shattering Jessica's delusion over the man's identity.

He straightened as the car braked to a halt, lifting the glass to his lips and at the same time taking a step forward out of the shadow of the veranda. Jessica sucked in a sharp breath as sunlight fell upon silky golden locks and smooth bronzed shoulders. He continued drinking as he walked slowly down the steps, taking deep swallows and seemingly unconscious of his quite extraordinary beauty.

A couple of drops of water fell from the base of the frosted glass onto his almost hairless chest, Jessica's fascinated eyes following them as they trickled down to pool in his navel, which was sinfully exposed above the low-slung white shorts.

Jessica found herself swallowing, her throat suddenly

dry. Her eyes dropped further as he continued his measured descent, taking in every inch of his leanly muscled legs. They lifted at last to once again encounter his face, no longer obscured by the glass.

It was as disturbingly attractive as the rest of him, with a strong straight nose, an elegantly sculptured jawline, bedroom blue eyes and a far too sexy mouth. As he drew nearer, Jessica's stunned fascination gradually turned to a simmering fury.

Hadn't seen thirty in many years, my foot! she thought angrily. Even if he did look young for his age, he could be no more than thirty-five. If that!

Before he reached the bottom step she'd flung open the car door and stepped out, drawing herself up to her full height and glaring scornfully into that now treacherously smiling face. No one had to tell Jessica what sort of man he was. She hadn't come down in the last shower.

His smile faltered, then faded, his narrowed blue gaze staring, first into her cold black eyes, then down over her stiffly held body and up again.

Was he taken aback by her obvious contempt for him? Had he imagined for one moment that he could fool her, too?

Jessica almost laughed. Sebastian Slade was everything she'd feared when she'd first heard of him. And possibly more.

Despite all this, she swiftly and sensibly decided to hide her feelings, smoothing the derision from her face and stepping forward with her hand politely stretched out. There was no need to be overtly rude to him. She knew the score now. Why make her stay more awkward than it would already be?

She would endure his undoubted hypocrisy for the next month then send him packing without anything to remember her by, except a few parting shots. Oh, yes, she would tell him what she thought of him on that final day. And she'd enjoy every word!

He hesitated to take her hand, staring at it for a few seconds before staring into her face. His expression reminded her of the way Aunt Lucy had stared at her that day. What was it about the way she looked that was so surprising? Okay, so she didn't look like her mother, but she was very like her father, who'd been tall, with dark eyes and hair.

Jessica was beginning to feel a little unnerved by his intense regard when Evie joined them, laughing.

'You should see the look on your face, Sebastian,' she said as she swept the empty glass out of his hand. 'Yes, Lucy's niece is a striking-looking woman, isn't she? Not exactly what you expected, eh what?'

'Not exactly,' he said, a rueful smile hovering about his sensually carved mouth.

She found herself glaring at that mouth and wondering caustically if it had pressed treacherous kisses to her aunt's lips. It would be naive of her to think that a woman in her fifties would not take a lover twenty years her junior. It happened a lot in the name of lust. Lust for a beautiful young male body on her aunt's part. Lust for money and material gain on Mr. Slade's.

'Welcome to Norfolk Island,' he said formally at last, taking her hand in his. 'And welcome to Lucy's Place. How do you like it?'

I'd like it a lot more, she thought crossly, *if you'd let go my hand. And if you'd go put some more clothes on.* Damn, but the man was breathtakingly attractive. On a rating of zero to ten, his sex appeal would measure twenty.

'It's lovely,' she said truthfully, but stiffly.

'Do you think you might change your mind about staying on and living here, then?'

'No, I can't see that happening,' she replied, despite feeling a definite tug at her heartstrings. Anyone would love to live in such a beautiful house. But a house did not make a home, and life on Norfolk Island was not for her, however sweet their customs.

Was that relief she glimpsed in his eyes, or disappointment? Actually, it looked more like frustration. Jessica's brain began to tick over. Did Mr. Slade have some secret agenda where she was concerned? Did he need more than a month to achieve his goal?

And what could that goal be? she puzzled. To move on to the next victim, perhaps? To seduce his dearly departed lover's heiress?

Jessica shuddered at the thought.

'She'll change her mind,' Evie said confidently, and moved up the steps. 'Her case is on the back seat, Sebastian,' she called over her shoulder. 'Flex your muscles and bring it inside. I'll go rustle up some lunch.'

At least he released her hand then. And moved away.

Jessica was annoyed with herself for letting him get under her skin, even a little. Still, she had to admit that his physical charisma was incredible. It was as well she was on her guard against him.

'I won't, you know,' she said tartly when he returned with her case.

'Won't what?'

'Stay on and live here. There's nothing you can say or do to change my mind.'

'What makes you think I'd *want* to change your mind?'

The coldness in his voice surprised her, as did the

scorn that flashed across his face. It was hardly the way a man would act if he had seduction on his mind.

'I promised Lucy I would make your month's stay as enjoyable as possible,' he went on, just as coldly, 'and that I would show you what the island has to offer. But I can see already you're not the sort of girl to appreciate simple things or a simple lifestyle, so I won't overtax myself playing persuader.'

'You're too kind,' she countered, matching his icy tone.

His top lip lifted slightly, just short of a sneer. 'Tell me, Miss Rawlins. What's the sum total of your reason for coming here? Are you interested at all in finding out about your heritage and your roots? Or is this simply a matter of money?'

Jessica began quivering with suppressed rage. 'Don't you dare presume to judge me, you...you *gigolo*!'

He actually dropped her case. It tumbled down the steps, but he made no move to try to retrieve it. He simply stood there, staring wide-eyed into her flushed face.

'Gigolo?' he exclaimed.

His shock was echoed by her own. Whatever had possessed her to say such a stupid thing! As true as it might be, it had been a tactless and very rude accusation. Still, having voiced her private beliefs, Jessica was not about to back down. Why should she when he'd virtually accused *her* of being a mercenary money-grabbing bitch?

'Are you saying you weren't my aunt's lover?' she asked scornfully. 'That you haven't been hanging around here for what you could get?'

'Good God. What a nasty piece of work you are!'

'Don't try to turn the tables on me, Mr. Slade,' she bit out. *'You're* the one described in my aunt's will as her loyal and loving companion, yet you must be twenty years younger than she was. *You're* the one who's wangled it so that you're still living here free of charge. I've no doubt you always did! And *you're* the one who inherits everything if I don't comply with my aunt's peculiar wishes. Are you saying you never made love to her? That you didn't worm your way into her affections with sex? That she didn't give you her car, and God knows what else, for services rendered?'

Jessica reeled under the chilling contempt in his arctic blue eyes. 'I'm going to forget you said that, because if I don't, I might be tempted to break my word to the nicest woman I've ever known. You might be her niece, but I can see you don't have a single gene of hers. No doubt you take after your pathetic parents!'

Jessica's face went bright red. 'You didn't even know my parents! And you certainly don't know *me*!'

His mouth opened to say something, then closed again. He looked away from her, his hands lifting to rake through his hair before looking back, a shuddering sigh emptying his lungs.

'Let's stop this right now,' he said with cool firmness. 'I have no intention of spending the next month exchanging verbal darts with you. Neither will I defend the relationship I had with your aunt, other than to say I never sought anything from her but her friendship, which I hope I gave back in kind.'

'Are you saying that you weren't her lover?' Jessica challenged.

His top lip curled with more contempt as his gaze swept over her. 'Would you believe me if I said no?'

'Try me.'

His cold gaze swept over her quite insultingly.

'No, I don't think I will,' he said at last with a derisive glitter in his eyes.

Jessica stiffened. 'Very funny. If you won't deny it, then I will have to presume that you were.'

'Believe what you like,' he replied with cold indifference.

'Oh, I will, Mr. Slade,' she said tartly. 'I will. As to *your* accusation that I'm only here for the money... I won't be holier than thou and say money isn't important to me. It is. But not to the extent you've implied. Still, I, too, see no need to defend myself. I'm not sure if you know this, but I had no idea I even *had* an aunt till recently, when she showed up at the hotel where I work.'

'Yes, I *do* know about that,' he said, surprising her.

'But...but I thought you didn't know of my existence till the will showed up.'

'I didn't know your full name and address till the will showed up. But I did know Lucy had found she had a niece named Jessica working in a hotel in Sydney, and that she'd left everything to you in her will. Lucy only spoke of you by your first name. I naturally assumed I would know all the necessary details once the will was read, but when Lucy died, I couldn't find the damned thing. It had slipped behind a drawer, you see.'

'Yes, the solicitor told me.'

'Frankly, Lucy told me only the barest of details about you. She didn't seem to want to talk about your one meeting. I was about to ring every hotel in Sydney when I came across the will.'

'Are you saying you can't tell me *why* Aunt Lucy left the hotel that day without really speaking to me?' Jessica asked painfully. 'You know, she stared at me like I was a ghost at first. I was called away for a few minutes, and when I returned she was gone. She hadn't even told me *her* last name, either, which was why *I* wasn't able to trace *her*.'

'I see. That explains a few questions I had myself, but no... I'm afraid I can't tell you why Lucy ran away from you. God only knows. Perhaps she was having trouble coming to terms with the guilt of never having looked up her sister before and seeing if she was all right. I think the news that Joanne was dead came as a dreadful shock to her.'

Jessica was shaking her head, her eyes dropping wearily to the ground. 'I don't understand any of it.'

A surprisingly gentle hand on her arm jerked her head upright. She was stunned by the momentary compassion in those beautiful blue eyes of his, and the confusion it stirred in her heart. Compassion was not something she was familiar—or comfortable—with. On top of that, it was not at all what she was expecting from *this* man.

'Of course you can't understand any of it,' he said with surprising sympathy. 'It's hard enough to understand what goes on in our own lives. Much more difficult to work out the lives of others. But you have a month to find some answers for your questions. I'll help as much as I can. Not that I have all the answers. But for now, why don't you come inside? It's hot out here, and Evie will be wondering where we are.'

Jessica automatically pulled back when he went to take her arm, feeling flustered by his suddenly solicitous attitude towards her. Such an about-face had to be viewed with some suspicion.

His frown carried frustration. 'There's no need to act like that. I was only trying to be friendly.'

'Why?' she demanded. 'A few minutes ago, you were calling me a nasty bit of work.'

'That was a few minutes ago. Maybe I've changed my mind about you since then.'

And maybe pigs might fly, she thought cynically, one of her eyebrows lifting in a sceptical arch.

A wry smile curved his mouth to one side, bringing her attention to those sensually carved lips, and where they might have been. The thought that he might have changed his mind about seducing her held an insidiously exciting aspect, one she would find hard to ignore.

But ignore it she would. She hadn't come here to fall victim to the slick, shallow charms of a man like Sebastian Slade, no matter how sexy he was.

'I see you still don't trust me,' he said dryly. 'Funnily enough, I can see your point of view. I dare say there are others on this island who think the same as you. I've just never cared what they thought. I stopped caring about what people thought of me some years ago.'

'Lucky ol' you,' she retorted tartly. 'Would we could all have the same privilege. Unfortunately, most of us have to live in the real world and work at a real job, which means we do have to worry what others think.'

'But you *don't* have to, Jessica,' he pointed out in a silky soft voice, which rippled down her spine like a mink glove. 'You don't have to live in the real world any more, or work at a real job, if you don't want to. Neither do you have to give a damn what people think. You can do what you like from this day forward.'

It was a wickedly seductive thought, provocatively delivered by a wickedly seductive man. She looked at him, her face a bland mask, while she battled to stop her mind from its appalling flights of fancy.

He was technically right, of course. If she invested her inheritance wisely she would never have to work again for the rest of her life, or kowtow to a boss. He was also right about her not having to worry about what other people thought, especially during the next month. Out here on this island, in this isolated house, she could do exactly as she pleased, and there was no one to judge or condemn.

Why was he pointing that out to her? She puzzled over this. Was it part of his seduction technique, to corrupt his victim with thoughts of a lifestyle of totally selfish and hedonistic behaviour?

He would have to do better than that, she thought with bitter amusement. She'd been seduced before by good-looking liars and had no intention of going that route again, no matter how stunningly this particular liar was put together.

'Let me tell you something, Mr. Slade,' she said coolly. 'I happen to like the real world, not to mention my real job. But thank you for explaining that I don't have to worry about what other people think of me here. I hope that includes you.'

He stared at her, and she would have loved to know what he was thinking. 'Touché,' he said at last, the smallest of wry smiles playing around his mouth. 'By the way, call me Sebastian, would you? Or Seb, if you prefer.'

'I prefer Sebastian,' she said crisply.

Which she did, actually. It also suited him very well. It was a strong name, yet sensual—like its owner. Not a modern name. There was nothing modern about Sebastian's looks. If he'd been an actor, he would never be cast as a business executive. He would, however, make a magnificent Viking prince, or a knight in King Arthur's court, or one of the Three Musketeers, with a feathered hat atop his flowing locks.

'Sebastian it will be, then,' he agreed nonchalantly. 'I'll just get your case.' He turned and walked with indolent grace down the steps to where it had fallen, his

bending over drawing his shorts tightly over his tantalisingly taut buttocks.

Jessica tried not to stare, but she was doomed to failure. Never had a man's body fascinated her so much
before. There again…it was a gorgeous body.

He straightened and turned, their eyes meeting as he
slowly mounted the steps. It wasn't just his body, she
conceded ruefully. Those eyes were like blue magnets,
drawing her, tempting her. And that mouth of his was
made strictly for sin.

Damn, but she hoped nothing she was thinking was
showing on her face.

Self-preservation had Jessica throwing him one of her
coolest looks before whirling and walking up the steps
and into her Aunt Lucy's beautiful home.

CHAPTER FOUR

THE house was even more beautiful inside than out. Over a hundred years old, Sebastian told her, but lovingly cared for and restored to retain its original old-world charm.

The use of Norfolk pine was extensive, from the polished timber floors to the stained wall panelling to the kitchen benches and cupboards. Very little of the furniture, however, was made from local wood.

Sebastian explained that most pieces had been shipped in from New Zealand and Australia and even England, and were made from a variety of woods. There were fine examples of oak and teak, mahogany and rosewood, walnut and cedar.

The bathrooms featured black marble from Devon, brought over in sailing boats a century before. The bedrooms were a delight to behold, with their carved four-poster beds and exquisitely delicate furnishings.

Everywhere Jessica looked there was lace in some form or other. Lace curtains and bedspreads, tablecloths and doilies. In pure whites and rich creams, the lace lent an old-world atmosphere and blended beautifully with the fine porcelain figurines that rested on the many ornamental side tables and shelves. Overhead, the light fittings were mainly brass. Underfoot, fine woven rugs in earthy colours took the chill off the floors.

It was a warm and wonderful home, with style and an air of contentment Jessica could only envy.

She felt guilty at the thought she might sell her aunt's property to someone who would not care for the home and its contents as her aunt obviously had. It would be a crime to disturb a single thing. Everything fitted together like a jigsaw puzzle. There wasn't a piece missing.

'What a perfect, perfect place,' she murmured as she wandered through one of the large living rooms, running an affectionate hand along the mantelpiece above the marble fireplace.

'It was Lucy's pride and joy,' Sebastian said.

Jessica's eyes moved reluctantly to where he'd stayed standing in the doorway, her suitcase at his feet.

She'd avoided looking at him too much during her grand tour of the house. Inside, he seemed even more naked than he had outside. And much sexier...if that were possible.

Jessica had been quite unnerved when they'd brushed shoulders once, a decidedly sexual quiver running through her at the physical contact. After that, she'd kept her distance. He seemed to keep his, too, for which she was grateful. She could think of nothing more embarrassing—or awkward—than his finding out she was in any way vulnerable to him.

'It's such a shame I have to sell it,' she said.

'Why do you have to sell it? Why not live here yourself?'

'It's not as easy as that, Sebastian,' she said stiffly. 'I have a life in Sydney. And a career.'

'You call slaving for someone else a career? You could make a real career out of running this place like Lucy did. She did very well yet she only opened the house for guests in the summer.'

'I wouldn't be very good at that type of thing.'

'Come now. The public relations manager of a big city hotel could run a place like this standing on her head. Now don't look so surprised. One of the things Lucy *did* tell me was what you did in Sydney, even if she didn't say where. She sounded very proud of you.'

'I see. Well it's not a matter of capability, Sebastian. It's a matter of what I enjoy doing. I enjoy being a public relations manager. I don't enjoy housekeeping.'

'Neither did Lucy. When she had guests, she had a girl come in every day to do the laundry and ironing, another to do the heavy cleaning and Evie to cook. Lucy's role was more of a hostess, though she did make breakfast in the mornings.'

'What did she do with herself all day?'

'She entertained her guests, in the main. Her friendly and relaxing style of companionship was one of the reasons the same people came back to stay here year after year. Lucy was a very calming person to be around. And then, of course, there was her garden. She spent a lot of time there, too. She loved her flowers. Do you like flowers, Jessica?'

'What woman doesn't like flowers? I can't say I'm much of a gardener, though. I've never had a garden.'

'You would here.'

'I didn't say I wanted one.'

'You didn't say you didn't, either.'

She sighed an exasperated sigh. 'Stop trying to change my mind, Sebastian. I don't want to run a guesthouse. I am not going to stay. I'm here for one month and one month only.'

He said nothing. Absolutely nothing. But his mouth tightened a little and she thought she saw scorn in his eyes.

Jessica bristled, resenting the feeling she was having to defend herself to this man all the time. She decided it was his turn to answer some questions.

'What else did Lucy tell you about me?' she demanded.

'Nothing much.' He shrugged. 'She said you looked and seemed very…efficient. That's about it. You must appreciate Lucy found out as little about you in your brief meeting as you did about her.'

He was lying. Aunt Lucy had told him something else, something that had made him stare at her when they'd first met. But it was clear he wasn't going to tell her. She felt quite frustrated with him. And totally frustrated with herself.

Dear God, it was as well he was on the other side of the room, for as she looked at him now, she felt the urge to reach out and touch, to see if his long golden hair was as silky as it seemed, to know if his bronzed skin was as satiny smooth as it looked.

The man was a menace! Why couldn't he have been rising sixty, with a paunch and a greying beard? she thought irritably. Why did he have to be a golden god with eyes one could drown in and a mouth to tempt even the most frigid virgin?

'Have you decided which bedroom you want to sleep in?' he asked abruptly.

Yours, came the wicked thought before she could stop it entering her mind.

Jessica took a deep, steadying breath. 'No,' she said. 'But not Lucy's. I wouldn't feel comfortable in Lucy's room.'

'Which leaves you four to choose from, since I have no intention of giving you mine.'

'It's hard to choose,' she said. 'From what I can remember they were all beautiful.'

'The view is better on the southern side,' he advised, 'and you get more breezes in the evening.'

'Which side is the southern side?'

'This side. *My* side. I'll put your case in the room next to mine, shall I?'

'Oh, er, all right.'

'Good.' He bent to pick up the heavy case, the movement highlighting the sleekly defined muscles in his chest and upper arms.

'I know you probably promised my aunt you would try to persuade me to stay, Sebastian,' she burst out, a type of panic invading her at the thought of spending a whole month in the bedroom next to his. 'But the truth is...I simply could not bear to live permanently on Norfolk Island.'

He straightened and looked at her with suppressed exasperation in his eyes. 'How do you know that? You haven't tried it.'

'You don't have to climb Mount Everest to know that it's freezing cold up there,' she said defensively.

'Meaning?'

'Life here is too slow for me. And far too quiet. I'd be bored in no time.'

His eyes locked with hers across the room, and she felt instantly breathless.

'You think so?' he said with a taunting softness.

'I *know* so.'

'You know nothing, Jessica,' he said with an almost weary sigh. 'Just as I knew nothing when I first came here. But I won't bore you by telling you about my experience. I can see Evie's quite wrong. You won't change your mind. Still, perhaps it's just as well. You really don't suit the island any more than it suits you.'

His eyes became cold again as they raked over her. 'No. You're much better suited to a career in Sydney. I dare say having to stay here for a whole month has inconvenienced you no end.'

Jessica resented the underlying contempt in his voice. Who was he to judge anyone? 'Yes, it has, actually,' she said curtly. 'I might have risked my job in dropping everything and coming at once.'

'Pardon me if my heart doesn't bleed for you. I'm sure your inheritance will more than compensate for any inconvenience. And if you lose your job, then what the hell? You'll survive till you get the next one.'

'You still believe all I care about is the money, don't you?'

'If the cap fits, wear it, Jessica.'

'I have not come just for the money!'

'Whatever you say.' His expression was distant, as though he didn't give a damn either way.

'Lunch in ten minutes!' Evie called from the depths of the house. 'I'll serve it out on the back veranda.'

'Fine, Evie,' Sebastian called down the hallway before turning to face Jessica. 'Let's get you along to your room,' he said briskly. 'You might like to shower and change before lunch. I know I do. I probably smell of fish. I threw away my T-shirt earlier because it was high as a kite, but I think I must still be on the nose a bit. I couldn't help but notice you run a mile every time I get too close.'

Jessica found some relief that this was what he thought. The last thing she wanted was for him to think she fancied him. My God, the last thing she'd wanted—or expected—was to fancy him at all!

She wasn't sure why she did, with the way he was treating her. Like she was a cold-hearted, ambitious bitch! Okay, so he was gorgeous looking, in a blond, bronzed surfie fashion, but she'd never been attracted to that type before, not even in her younger days. She'd always gone for dark, intensely passionate types, the ones who couldn't stop looking at you, who flattered you like mad and were always over you like a rash as soon as they got you alone.

Jessica's previous lovers had always rushed her into the bedroom before she could draw breath, and silly lonely love-struck fool that she was, she'd never thought to say no, even when the bells didn't ring and the stars didn't explode.

She'd long come to terms with the fact that while the men she'd fallen in love with had been passionate types, they hadn't been the most skilled lovers in the world. They had been impatient for their own pleasure, quick and selfish, takers, not givers.

She stared at Sebastian as she crossed the room and wondered what kind of lover *he* was. Which led her to the question of whether he had a girlfriend somewhere on the island.

She didn't like that idea. Not one bit. It was a perversely telling moment.

'I'll use the bathroom on the other side of the house,' he said, 'if that's what you're frowning about.'

Jessica frowned some more till she remembered none of the bedrooms had ensuites. Each side of the house had a bathroom and separate toilet, with a third powder room and toilet coming off the hallway near the living rooms.

'I think that's a good idea,' she said coolly. 'Perhaps you should always use that bathroom for the duration of my stay here. That way we won't have to worry about sharing, or running into each other accidentally in the bathroom.'

And I won't have to worry about drooling over you too much.

He stared at her for a moment, then shrugged. 'Okay. If that's what you want.'

'What I want, Sebastian,' she said as she followed him into the bedroom he'd chosen for her, 'is for you to tell me the truth.'

He placed her suitcase on the ottoman at the foot of her four-poster bed, then glanced at her, his face annoyingly bland. 'About what?'

'About everything.'

'Everything?'

'You know what I mean, so don't play dumb. It doesn't suit you.'

'What if I think you're not ready to know... everything?' he said with irritating calm.

'What gives you the right to make such a judgment?' she countered frustratedly. 'You know, you have a habit of making ill-founded judgments. You accused me earlier of not wanting to find out about my heritage. Then, just now, you virtually accused me for a second time of only coming here for the money. You were wrong on both counts. I would have survived quite well without Aunt Lucy's money. But I doubt I'll survive without knowing the facts surrounding my mother's flight from her family, and her pretending they didn't exist, and vice versa. So stop telling me what I think and what I feel! You don't know anything about me. Not the real me. You probably never will.'

His eyebrows shot ceilingwards. Jessica wasn't sure if he was impressed by her outburst, or taken aback. Frankly, she didn't care. She was too mad to care.

'I also want to know where you fit into all this,' she swept on heatedly. 'Okay, so you refuse to tell me if you and my aunt were lovers, but I still want to know who in hell you are, and how you came to live here, and why Aunt Lucy put you in her will in such a peculiar back-handed fashion?'

His smile was wry. 'Thems a lot of questions, Jess. It would take me all day and all night to answer them.'

His calling her Jess almost distracted her from her mission. For a few disarming seconds she took some perverse pleasure from the possibility that it meant he was beginning to believe her. Or perhaps even *like* her.

But just as swiftly she pushed such silly considerations aside and put her mind on why she was here. For it certainly wasn't to become involved with a man like Sebastian Slade, who was at best a bit of a beach bum, at worst, a gold-digging gigolo.

'I *have* all day and all night,' she said firmly. 'And so do you, by the look of things.'

'I work in the afternoons.'

'You...work?' Her face and voice must have shown her surprise.

'Yes. Did you think I just lazed around every day, doing nothing but fish?'

Pretty well, came the dryly cynical thought.

'What on earth do you do?' she asked. Maybe his idea of work and her idea of work were two different things.

'I write.'

'Write,' she repeated dully, as though she'd lost her brain power. But frankly, he looked about as far removed from a writer as one could get.

'What do you write?'

'I'm working on a novel.'

'You mean you're a novelist? You earn money from writing books?'

'I hope to. A publisher has already accepted my story on the first two hundred pages plus a synopsis. I've completed a further four hundred and have about fifty to go. Since my deadline is the end of this month, I'm sure you must appreciate I can't have an afternoon off at this stage.'

'What's it about, this novel of yours?'

His sigh was a little weary. 'Jessica, for pity's sake, you never open your mouth except to ask more questions. I could be here forever if I started answering them now. Have a quick shower and change into something cooler. You look hot. I'll tell you about my book over lunch. Then tonight at dinner, and afterwards, I'll try to answer all your other questions.'

'You won't hold anything back?' she asked. 'Promise?'

'I promise to put myself at your total disposal till you are well and truly satisfied. Fair enough?'

He could not possibly have meant any double entendre within that statement, but still, his words put perturbing pictures into her mind. Pictures of her staying all night in his bed, being made love to over and over, no sexual stone unturned till she lay exhausted and thoroughly sated in his arms.

Jessica swallowed, then struggled to find her voice. 'F-fair enough.'

He smiled at her then, an unconsciously sensual smile, which made her feel suddenly weak at the knees.

'See you at lunch,' he said. 'I'll tell Evie to hold the food for another five minutes, but don't be long.'

CHAPTER FIVE

JESSICA managed to find her way to the back veranda in just over ten minutes. Sebastian was already there, slightly more dressed than earlier in multicoloured board shorts and a bright blue singlet the same colour as his eyes. His hair hung darkly damp onto his shoulders in gentle waves.

He looked deliciously cool, hunkily handsome and irritatingly relaxed, leaning back in a deep cane chair, his bare feet up on the veranda railing.

'Great view, isn't it?' he said as she settled herself in an adjacent chair, a glass-topped cane table between them. He didn't even look her way.

Jessica's automatic pique was telling. She'd told herself she hadn't dressed to attract him, that she'd chosen to wear her white cheesecloth outfit simply because it didn't need ironing, and not because it was the most feminine thing she'd brought with her.

Now she gazed at her clothes with a rueful acceptance of the truth. The skirt flowed in sensually soft folds to mid-calf, the matching shirt falling loosely from her shoulders to her hips, its thin white material showing tantalising glimpses of the half-cup lace bra she was wearing underneath, one that pressed her breasts up and together. She'd deliberately left the top two of the mother-of-pearl buttons open at the neck, forming a deep

V neckline, which displayed a good inch or two of cleavage.

Jessica felt frustration at her own stupidity, and relief that the object of this unwanted sexual attraction was indifferent to her appearance. Still, she was thankful she hadn't had time to change her hair. Leaving her hair down might have delivered a none too subtle message.

With a small sigh she crossed her legs, noting as she did that her toenail polish was chipped. Embarrassed— she was a perfectionist about her personal grooming— she uncrossed her legs and swung them underneath her chair to hide her feet.

It was only then that she really took in the view Sebastian had remarked upon.

My God, but it *was* magnificent! Rolling green hills in the forefront, framed by stately Norfolk Island pines. The Pacific Ocean in the distance, a great expanse of blue-green water broken by two small craggy islands, which looked deserted. Above, cotton wool clouds were scattered across a deep aqua sky.

'There aren't any boats on the horizon,' she commented, surprised. In Sydney, you could rarely look out at the ocean and not see a boat on the horizon.

'We're not on any shipping line here,' Sebastian replied. 'The only boat you'll ever see other than local fishing boats is the occasional supply ship. It's quite an event when one shows up. Everyone goes down to the pier to watch the unloading.'

Wow, Jessica thought dryly, trying not to show what she felt about that on her face.

Sebastian laughed. 'You think that's about as interesting as watching grass grow, don't you?'

What was the point in lying to him?

She threw a rueful glance his way. 'Something like

that,' she admitted. 'But maybe I'm wrong. If a boat comes in while I'm here, take me down to watch for a while.'

'All right. I'll do that. Ah, here's Evie with some brain food.'

'It's nothing fancy,' Evie said as she carried a tray over and proceeded to put a plate each on the table between them. 'Just some club sandwiches, followed by banana cake and tea. Or coffee, if you'd prefer.' She directed the last remark towards Jessica.

'Tea would be just fine,' she said, smiling. The only time she liked coffee was first thing in the mornings and after dinner at night. 'This looks delicious.' Jessica picked up the long sesame-seed-covered roll filled with cold meat and salad and took a bite. 'Aren't you having one, Evie?'

'I already did, in the kitchen. Sebastian, you've let provisions really run down in the freezer. I'll have to do some shopping this afternoon before I can produce a decent meal tonight.'

'There's plenty of trumpeter in the fridge,' he said, and Jessica wondered what trumpeter was.

'We can't eat fish every night,' Evie told him, thereby solving the mystery. 'And I need some fresh vegetables.'

'Have you enough money to buy what you need, Evie?' Jessica asked. 'I'll pay you back tomorrow when I go to the bank. I didn't carry all that much cash with me on the plane.'

'I'll fix her up with some money,' Sebastian offered.

'Certainly not,' Jessica snapped. 'The will said you were to live here free of charge, and that's exactly what you'll do.'

'For pity's sake don't start arguing, you two,' Evie protested. 'That would be the last thing Lucy wanted. I'll pay for the food and Jessica can pay me back. Now eat up and I'll go get the banana cake and tea.'

'Forceful woman,' Sebastian said after Evie disappeared.

'She's a very nice lady,' Jessica defended.

'I was talking about you.'

'Oh.' Her head turned and their eyes met over their rolls.

He was looking at her now. *Really* looking at her, drinking her in, his eyes starting on hers and travelling slowly downwards, past her suddenly drying mouth, down the V neckline to where her swelling breasts were forming an even more impressive cleavage. Her nipples suddenly felt like hard pebbles, pressing against the lace confines of her bra. Her heart was thudding heavily behind her ribs.

Thank God I'm not given to blushing, she thought with growing irritation.

Her chin lifted instinctively in defiance of the effect he had on her. He wasn't even looking at her with desire in his eyes. If anything, there was a rueful edge to his appraisal, as though he recognised her physical attractiveness but was totally immune.

Not like you, came the voice of self-disgust. *He only has to look at you and your veins fill with a liquid heat.*

She looked away quickly and busied herself eating so that by the time Evie returned with a tray of tea and cake, she'd finished her roll and gathered her composure.

'That's what I like to see,' Evie said happily. 'An appreciative eater. Look, I might dash off to the shops now. Just stack the dirty things in the dishwasher after you've finished. Be back by five. Oh, and I don't want to hear you two have been squabbling while I'm gone.'

The atmosphere between them seemed to thicken appreciably with Evie's departure, though maybe it was Jessica's imagination. Perhaps it was simply because it was difficult to talk with mouthful after mouthful of banana cake. Truly, the square Evie had given her was enormous. The cake was delicious but quite heavy. One needed two cups of tea to wash it down.

'Having trouble with the cake?' Sebastian asked, breaking the awkward silence that had developed.

'A little. I'm not as hungry as I thought I was. My stomach must still be on Sydney time.' She'd had to put her watch forward two and a half hours before leaving the plane. On daylight saving time, it was only ten-thirty in the morning back home.

'You'll soon adjust. Well, do you want to start with the questions? I can give you half an hour before I have to get back to work.'

'That's not very long.'

'Then don't waste any of it,' he said quite sharply.

Surprise at his tone sent her eyebrows arching. 'Why are you angry at me?'

'I'm not,' he denied.

Oh, yes, you are, she decided. *You definitely are. I wonder why?*

'Get on with the questions, Jessica,' he drawled, his anger under control if his cold eyes were anything to go by.

'Very well,' she returned tersely. 'Why don't you tell me about yourself to begin with? Give me a brief autobiography.'

His laugh was disbelieving. 'Sorry. I'm not in the habit of telling a perfect stranger my entire life story.'

'But I'm not a perfect stranger!'

'Of course you are. I know as little about you as you know about me.'

'But...but...'

'Stop stammering. It doesn't suit you. Now do you want to know about my book or do you want to start giving me the third degree about your aunt and myself again?'

Jessica opened her mouth then snapped it shut. She eyed Sebastian closely, all her doubts about his relationship with her aunt resurfacing with a vengeance. She suspected she could ask questions till the cows came home, but that didn't mean he would tell her the truth. About anything. All she could do was ask away and watch his body language.

'How did you come to meet Aunt Lucy?' was her first question.

His shoulders visibly relaxed at the question, showing he had been a little tense over what she might ask. 'I came here for a holiday three years ago,' he said lightly, 'and I simply stayed on.'

'*You* came here for a holiday? To Lucy's Place?'

'Yes. What's so surprising about that?'

'Were you alone?'

'I certainly was.'

'But why?'

'Why was I alone?'

'No, why did you choose Norfolk Island, if you were alone? It's not the sort of place a good-looking young man would go for a holiday on his own.'

'Firstly, I wasn't all that young. I was thirty-five at the time.'

Jessica was startled. Thirty-five three years ago. That made him thirty-eight now. He didn't look a day over thirty, even if there were some lines around his eyes she hadn't noticed before.

'I wanted to get right away from the rat-race,' he went

on. 'I'd been working very hard for years and I was burnt out.'

'Working hard at what?'

'As a dealer in an American-owned bank in Sydney. If you know anything about dealing, and about American banks, you'll know how stressful such a job can be. On top of that, I was having personal problems.'

'What sort of personal problems?'

He flashed her a look that indicated that was not a question he wanted to answer. 'Money troubles,' he said brusquely. 'Amongst other things.'

'You still had enough for a fancy holiday,' she fired at him. 'This place wouldn't come cheap.'

He seemed taken aback for a second before smiling a slow smile. 'I managed,' he said.

'How long was the holiday for?'

'Three weeks.'

'At the end of which Aunt Lucy invited you to stay on, free of charge?'

'Not exactly. A couple of days after I arrived I fell ill with a virus. Apparently that happens sometimes when workaholics suddenly stop work. Perversely, their immune systems go down, instead of up, and they get sick. I was in bed for a week, then spent the rest of the three weeks recuperating. I had barely enough energy to do more than read a book. Lucy felt sorry for me and offered me another three weeks holiday, free of charge.'

'Which you jumped at.'

'Naturally. Wouldn't you?'

'I suppose so. So what happened at the end of that three weeks? Did Aunt Lucy invite you to stay on indefinitely, free of charge?'

'No, of course not. But by then I'd fallen in love with

Norfolk Island and wanted to stay, so I offered my services to your aunt in exchange for my bed and board.'

Jessica's eyebrows arched and Sebastian scowled.

'You have a dirty mind, do you know that?'

'I'm merely trying to imagine what kind of services a big city banker could offer my aunt. Financial consultant and adviser, perhaps?'

'No, a painter, Miss Suspicious.'

Her eyebrows shot up further. 'Painter? What do you mean? Do you paint portraits?'

'No, walls. Your aunt happened to mention she was going to hire someone to paint the house inside and out during the winter break. She never had guests in the house from the middle of May till the middle of September. Since by then April was already fast drawing to a close, I suggested she hire me to do it in exchange for my board.'

He chuckled at the memory. 'I said I'd painted before. Which I had...technically. I painted a bike once when I was a kid. I figured it didn't take a genius to paint flat surfaces and that I could learn on the job. I admit I was a bit slow at first, but frankly, I think I did a better job than a professional painter would have, simply because I cared about the place so much.'

'You did a good job,' she had to admit. It was the first thing she'd noticed about the place—the splendid paintwork.

Sebastian gave her a look of mock shock. 'Careful now, Miss Rawlins, that almost sounded like a compliment. Next thing you know, you'll start believing I had no ulterior motive in staying on here.'

Her returning look was droll. 'As much as you'll start believing I've come here for my health, and not my inheritance.'

This time, his laugh sounded almost amused. 'True, but perhaps, in the interests of Evie's peace of mind, we should at least agree to be polite to each other.'

'I *am* being polite, believe me.'

'God help me if you ever decide to get vicious.'

Jessica pulled a face at him. 'So how come you started writing a novel?'

'That was Lucy's idea. She said I should do something with my brain to stop it atrophying. She'd noticed how much I liked to read so she suggested I try my hand at writing a novel. I scoffed at the idea at first; said I was a typical male who only ever used the right side of his brain. Or is it the left?'

He frowned.

Damn, but he was even gorgeous-looking when he frowned.

'Whatever,' he continued, shrugging. 'The non-creative, non-communicating side. You know what I mean.'

'Indeed, I do,' she said dryly. Most of the men she'd ever known had lacked creativity and communication. They hadn't even been good liars!

She surveyed Sebastian's sexy face and body and thought *he'd* make a good liar. A woman would be too busy lusting after him to notice the bull he was feeding her. Poor Aunt Lucy would not have stood a chance!

'No one was more surprised than me to find I had a real knack for it,' he was saying. 'Moreover, I enjoyed it. That winter was marvellous. I used to paint every morning, write every afternoon and play games with Lucy every evening.'

Jessica barely had time to react before Sebastian laughed.

'Yes, I appreciate how that sounded. Sorry, but I still

can't satisfy your craving for decadence. Lucy was a
game addict. Cards, board games, word puzzles, cross-
words. I'm sure you've noticed there are no television
sets at Lucy's Place. Lucy claimed people came here to
get away from that sort of thing. She entertained herself
and others with simpler, more old-fashioned pastimes.'

Jessica *hadn't* noted the lack of television. Now she
was quietly appalled. Television had become her main
backup for companionship and entertainment over the
years. She could not imagine life without it!

'By the time I'd finished painting the house,' Sebastian
went on, 'I'd told my story idea and received an advance,
so I asked Lucy if I could stay on till I'd finished the
book.'

'Free of charge still?' Jessica asked archly.

'Of course not. Lucy was kind, but no fool. Renting
out rooms was her source of income. Though I admit she
did give me a reduced rate for being a longstanding
guest.'

'As well as her loyal and loving companion,' Jessica
added dryly.

His glance was sharp. 'Back to that again, are we?'

'Not just now. Are you a good writer?'

'I think so.'

'Are you going to make a fortune out of your book?'

'Probably. It's a damned good book.'

She had to laugh. 'I see modesty is not one of your
virtues.'

'Nor yours,' he said, his eyes dropping to her cleavage.

Jessica pulled another face at him.

'Don't take offence. There's nothing wrong with being
proud of one's...achievements. You've obviously done
very well for yourself. I take it your childhood was
poor?'

Her astonishment showed in her face.

'Takes one to know one,' he drawled.

'You were poor as a child, too?'

'Dirt poor.'

Jessica digested that for a good minute or two. If he was anything like herself, then financial security would mean a lot to him. Perhaps that was why he was quick to think badly of her, because he himself put money above all else.

There was a time when Jessica had been ruthlessly ambitious in her aims to get ahead so that she would never be poor again. Now, she was content to do a good job and be paid well for it.

'What happened to all the money you earned as a dealer?' she asked. Jessica had dated a dealer once and knew the sort of salary they commanded, not to mention the bonuses they received.

'I invested it.'

'Badly, I presume.'

He chuckled. 'I could have done better.'

Which meant he'd lost it all. She could understand how that happened. Dealers were basically gamblers who usually only played with other people's money. It seemed Sebastian had started playing with his own, with dire results.

She was surprised that he wasn't more devastated. Maybe he had been, but selling his book had helped him pick up the pieces. Maybe that was one of the reasons he was so grateful to Aunt Lucy—because she'd put him on the road to a second fortune. And maybe that was why he wasn't concerned over not being left anything in her will. Because he believed he would soon be pretty rich himself.

And maybe I'm guessing all wrong, Jessica thought ruefully.

'What kind of investment was it?' she asked. 'The money market? Futures?'

His blue eyes flashed with sudden irritation. 'Must we talk about money?' he flung at her. 'If there's one thing I've learnt since coming to Norfolk Island it's that money doesn't make you happy. Far from it. Let's just say I invested in the property market in the wrong place at the wrong time. I wasn't the only optimistic idiot who got his fingers burnt, but I sure as hell can guarantee I'm the best adjusted to the consequences of my greed and stupidity. I haven't thought about those bad investments since coming here, and I don't want to now.'

Jessica raised her eyebrows. Hard to believe that a man who'd once been dirt poor could dismiss being broke so easily, or pretend he could be happy without any money at all! Maybe he was just saying that because he was on the verge of making a stack more with his book. Or maybe he'd already lined his pockets with cash gifts from Lucy over the past three years.

Jessica felt frustrated that she couldn't simply ask and know she'd get a straight answer. Still, she wasn't about to let him totally off the hook.

'Very well,' she said. 'We'll talk of other things. How would you describe your relationship with my aunt?'

His glare carried exasperation. 'I thought I'd already made myself clear on that score. We were friends. She helped me and I helped her. It was a give-and-take relationship. We enjoyed each other's company. We liked each other. It was as simple as that.'

He still hadn't denied he'd taken her to bed, she noted wryly. It seemed he wasn't going to, either. He was going to let her stew about it. Jessica decided to approach the question from a different angle.

'Why didn't she leave you something in her will, Sebastian? Why leave everything to me? She didn't even know me, whereas you and she were obviously very... close.'

'You were still her niece. Her flesh and blood. It was right that she leave everything to you.'

'You don't resent it?'

'Why should I?'

'You might be forgiven for expecting some kind of legacy yourself.'

'She did leave me a legacy.'

Jessica was taken aback. 'Surely you're not talking about the car!'

'No, I'm talking about my soul.'

'Your *soul*?'

'That's right. When I came here I'd totally lost mine. She gave it back to me.'

'But...but...'

'I can appreciate your confusion, Jessica. *And* your suspicion. But I strongly suggest you stop trying to make me fit the role you've selected for me in your city-cynical mind. You'll be much happier if you do. Now I think it's time for me to get to work,' he pronounced firmly.

'But you haven't told me anything about your book yet,' she blurted out, though her mind was still on his last remarks. Had she been misjudging him? Was she being cynical?

'There's not much to tell, really. It's an adventure action novel set partly on this island at the time of the convict settlement last century. When I take you sight-seeing tomorrow morning, I'll take you down to the old gaol and explain the characters and the plot. Then it will make more sense.'

But nothing else is going to make sense, she thought bitterly as she watched him stand up and start stacking the plates. *Not my aunt's actions. Or yours. Or mine.*

Why did she have to be so attracted to him, against all the dictates of common sense? Why? Dear God, the thought of spending the whole morning with him tomorrow, alone, doing things lovers and honeymooners did on this island, was already sending her into a spin.

Once again, her eyes were drawn to the classical lines of his perfect face and perfect body, and the unconscious sensuality of his movements. His hands moved with a fluid grace, his fingers long and elegant, his fingernails spotlessly clean and neatly clipped.

Yet for all that, there was a primitive edge about him. A sense of the wild and untamed.

His lack of clothes, she supposed. Plus his long hair.

She watched it fall forward as he leaned over the table towards her, her eyes following his hands as they lifted to impatiently rake it from his face. The image came of her own hands sliding into his hair, of her drawing his mouth down to hers, then down to her breasts. Then lower...

Her stomach twisted with a raw jab of desire, and she almost moaned out loud.

God, but she had to get away from him, had to get him out of her sight.

'I'll finish that,' she offered as she jumped to her feet. 'You go back to your writing.'

She reached out to take the pile of plates, but in her haste their fingers brushed together, which was the last thing she wanted. It took all her willpower not to snatch her hand away. But the contact still sent a shudder rippling through her. The hair on the back of her neck and arms stood on end.

When her eyes flew to his face in panic, Jessica was stunned to catch a blazing blue gaze glaring at her.

It wasn't desire heating his eyes, however.

It was resentment, a bitter burning resentment.

He hid it quickly. But not quickly enough.

He said a brusque thank-you, turned and walked into the house before she could blink, leaving her staring after him.

So he *did* resent her over the will, she realised with a rush of...what? Disappointment? Dismay?

My God, that was telling, wasn't it? She'd almost begun to believe his assertion that he was an innocent party in all this, that he'd come here, shattered by some sort of personal crisis, then had the pieces put together by dear kind Aunt Lucy, after which he'd stayed on, stony-broke, yet wanting nothing from this lonely and very wealthy widow but friendship.

Silly Jessica. When was she going to learn that men lied when it came to sex and money? Of course Sebastian had been Aunt Lucy's lover. Only a fool would believe otherwise. And of course he'd received presents from her. But they hadn't been enough, had they? He'd wanted it all. But he hadn't got it all. A long-lost niece had popped up at the last minute to snatch his hard-won inheritance away from him.

It was no wonder he resented her.

So why had he bothered to lie to her? Why had he been so nice on the telephone, but not once she arrived? Perhaps he *had* been planning to seduce her, only she hadn't turned out to be quite so gullible as Aunt Lucy. He'd taken one look at her and known he had no chance in hell of conning such a city-smart broad.

Which was so ironic, it was almost funny!

Oh, if only he knew!

Jessica shuddered with self-disgust. How could she want a man to make love to her, suspecting he was nothing but a cold-blooded con man? She'd heard that everyone had a dark side, but this was the first time she'd encountered hers. In the past, she'd made love to assuage her loneliness or to feel loved. The feelings she had for Sebastian had little to do with loneliness or love, and everything to do with lust.

It was as well he wasn't out to seduce her, she realised ruefully. Lord knows what would happen if he made a pass at her. Jessica didn't like suffering from a case of unrequited lust—it was distracting and disturbing—but she was determined to ignore it. Maybe in a couple of days, it would wear off, once she got used to Sebastian's incredible sex appeal.

Meanwhile she would concentrate on the reason she was here. Finding out about her roots. She'd almost forgotten why she had come for a moment. Sebastian had made her forget. He was a menace, all right.

She wandered to her bedroom and began unpacking. She hoped Evie would come back a little earlier than five o'clock. Jessica was impatient to ask her some questions about her mother. Sebastian might know a few things Lucy had told him, but Evie had known Jessica's family for forty years!

God, but it would be good to finally find out what had happened all those years ago; good to have the jigsaw that had been jumbling in her mind fit together into a cohesive pattern.

She hoped Evie had most of the answers. Then she wouldn't have to spend too much time questioning Sebastian after dinner tonight. The less time she spent with him, the better!

CHAPTER SIX

EVIE arrived just after four-thirty, and Jessica trailed after her into the kitchen like a hungry puppy. She was hungry, all right, hungry for company and for answers for her ever-increasing curiosity.

It had been lonely lying on her bed all afternoon, unable to sleep, unable to do a damned thing. Her mind had been too active to read. If only there'd been a television to watch, to distract her growing agitation.

'I'm so glad you're back,' she said, and began helping Evie unpack the bags of groceries and other provisions.

'Hasn't Sebastian been keeping you company?'

'He disappeared into his room after lunch to write. I haven't seen hide nor hair of him since.'

Evie tut-tutted. 'He's a bit of a tiger where that book of his is concerned, but he could have put it aside on your first day here.'

'No matter,' Jessica said lightly. 'I unpacked and had a little lie-down. I've been up since four this morning. I had to be at the airport at five.'

'Goodness! It'll be early to bed for you tonight then, lovie.'

Jessica had to struggle to blank out another of those dark thoughts. 'Would you mind if I asked you a few things about my family while you work, Evie?' she said quickly.

'No, of course not. I've been wondering when you

were going to. I gather you didn't even know you had a family on Norfolk Island, am I right?'

'Yes. Mum always said she had no family, that she'd been dumped on a doorstep when she was a baby and had been brought up an orphan in a state institution.'

Evie shook her head. 'That was wicked of her,' she muttered. 'Just wicked.'

'She must have had her reasons,' Jessica defended. 'How old was she when she ran away from home, do you know?'

'Mmm. Must have been only seventeen. She hadn't long been home from school on the mainland after doing her higher school certificate. I remember Lucy toyed with the idea of her repeating because she'd been a year younger than most of her classmates.'

'Isn't there a high school here, on the island?' Jessica asked.

'Yes, right up to year twelve now. But in those days, kids could only attend school to year ten. If they wanted to go further, they were sent to boarding school, either over in Brisbane or Sydney. Joanne went to Sydney and came home with a real craving for a faster life than on Norfolk Island.'

Jessica could understand that. 'Do you think that's why she left home? Because she wanted to live in Sydney?'

'I really don't know. I only know she and Lucy had a big fight over something and Joanne took off, never to return. We all thought it was a rotten thing to do, because Lucy was getting married the following week and Joanne was supposed to be her bridesmaid. The wedding went ahead, but it was a pretty sombre affair.'

'I wonder what the fight was about?'

Evie shrugged. 'I dare say it was probably a teenager

rebellion thing, although I got the feeling she wasn't thrilled with Lucy getting married. Or maybe it was Bill she didn't like. I saw them arguing one day on the side of the road, and Joanne actually pushed Bill over. That's the sort of thing she would do. She had a temper and a half.'

Jessica could hardly believe what she was hearing. The woman she'd known had had no spirit. No fight at all. It was like she was hearing about a different person.

'No doubt she argued with Lucy over something and things were said that shouldn't have been said and pride prevented both of them from ever backing down later. Things like that can happen in families. Whatever it was, Lucy refused to speak of her.'

'As Mum refused to speak of Aunt Lucy. I wish I knew what they fought over.'

'I don't think we'll ever know that, now that Lucy's gone.'

'Maybe she told Sebastian.'

'I don't think so. He certainly never said anything to me about it, not even when he told me about you coming and all. And he would have, if he'd known something.'

Jessica wasn't too sure about that. A couple of times, she'd had the feeling Sebastian was keeping things from her.

'How much older was Lucy than my mother?' she asked.

'Let's see now. About five or six years, I think.'

'Five or six years...' Jessica mulled over the figures for a few moments. Her mother had been thirty-eight when she died eight years ago, which meant she would have been forty-six if she'd been alive today. Aunt Lucy, then, had only been fifty-two or fifty-three when they'd met a few weeks ago, younger than she'd looked. Of course, her illness would have made her look older.

'What did my grandmother die of, by the way?' she asked. 'She couldn't have been all that old.'

'She wasn't. It was tragic. Really tragic. She was flown over to Sydney for a simple operation and had a bad reaction to the anaesthetic.'

'And my grandfather? He's dead too, isn't he?'

Evie sighed. 'When his wife died, he promptly turned round and drank himself to death, as if that's what his poor daughters needed. Another dead parent.'

'That's how my *mother* died!' Jessica gasped. 'From drink.'

Evie's face was all sympathy. 'Oh, you poor love. I didn't realise. Lucy said she'd passed away from some disease. I just assumed it was cancer, too.'

'No, she died of liver and kidney failure. She'd been an alcoholic for years. You know, they say that runs in families,' she added, frowning, concerned that she might have inherited an addictive personality.

'What runs in families?' Sebastian said as he stalked into the kitchen and began filling up the kettle.

'Alcoholism,' Jessica admitted stiffly, wishing he'd stayed in his damned room. 'Both my grandfather and my mother drank themselves to death. Present thinking is that it's an inheritable disease.'

'What rot!' Sebastian snorted. 'Weak people just say that as an excuse. But you don't have to start worrying, Jessica. There's not a weak bone in your body.'

His sardonic tone suggested she'd just been criticised, not complimented. 'Another of your snap judgments, Sebastian?'

'An observation grounded in experience,' he retorted.

'Any woman of your age who's reached executive level in the hotel world in Sydney is made of steel.'

'Oh, good Lord!' Evie exclaimed crossly. 'I thought you two would get on like a house on fire. Instead, you keep sniping at each other. Heaven knows why!'

'Sebastian thinks all I'm interested in is Aunt Lucy's money,' Jessica said defensively. 'Just because I don't want to live here. Just because I'm going to sell.'

'Sell?' Evie repeated faintly. 'She's really going to sell?' She directed her question to Sebastian.

'As of this moment, yes,' he answered dryly.

'But...but this house has been in your family for over a hundred years!' Evie protested, her eyes swinging to Jessica. 'Your great-great-grandfather built it. He was one of the original Pitcairn Islanders who came here to settle the island after the convicts left. This land was a peppercorn grant given to your family by Queen Victoria herself, and you're just going to sell it?' She began shaking her head, her round shoulders sagging. 'Poor Lucy. She'd turn in her grave if she knew.'

'But...but...' Jessica struggled to say something. After all, this was the first she'd heard of any of this. She'd had no idea, no idea at all. Why hadn't she been told? Why had her mother kept her from knowing her family and learning to appreciate her heritage?

It was suddenly all too much. Tears filled her eyes, and she had to battle hard to control a wild mixture of feelings, not the least a deep dismay.

Sebastian's hands on her shoulders startled her out of her wretchedness. She'd had no idea he'd moved across the room to where she was standing.

'You shouldn't be so hard on her, Evie,' he said gently, turning her and cradling her against his chest. 'It's not her fault. She didn't know any of this. Lucy should

have told her. Lucy should have told her a lot of things,
I think, and not left it up to us. There, there, Jess, don't
cry.'

Jessica wasn't crying any more, had stopped soon after
he'd taken her in his arms. She wasn't thinking too
clearly, or breathing, aware of nothing but Sebastian's
hands, one cupping the back of her head, the other stroking rhythmically down her spine. Her face was turned so
that her ear covered his deeply thudding heart.

Did it pick up its beat as he held her?

It seemed so, but probably didn't.

When he went to pull away, her arms snaked around
his waist and held him close, wickedly revelling in the
feel of his hard male body against hers. Her darker side
had momentarily taken control, and the pleasure was
mind-blowing.

But such pleasure always had a price. The price of
peace. Jessica knew that she would pay for these moments of weakness. And pay dearly.

She could see herself now, lying awake at night, longing for more, longing to slip into his room, then slide
between the sheets of his bed, longing to make love to
him as she'd never made love to any man before....

The fantasy was so strong in her mind that her lips
parted, sending a hot, shuddering breath across his thinly
covered chest. He flinched under it, bringing Jessica back
to the reality of what she was doing, hugging a man who
didn't want to be hugged any longer.

She wrenched herself out of his arms with a strangled
sob.

'I'm sorry,' she said gruffly, hoping and praying he
took her flushed face for embarrassment. He was staring
at her, but she had no idea what he was thinking. 'I...I'm
not myself at the moment,' she stammered. 'I...I think

I'll go back to my room and lie down for a while. I'm terribly tired and I have a lot of thinking to do. Will…will you excuse me?'

Other than holding her by force, he really had no option but to let her blunder to her room. Jessica did just that, shutting the door behind her and leaning against it as she sucked in breath after ragged breath of much-needed air.

Dear God, what was happening to her? It wasn't as if she was the type of girl who'd ever been sex mad. Far from it. The way Sebastian kept affecting her was *way* outside her normal range of experience with men. When she'd been in his arms, she'd been consumed by a need so intense she could not begin to describe it.

It was insane! And very distressing.

Her head dropped to her hands and she wept, her tears almost despairing. She'd never felt so alone in all her life. Or so confused. Or so wretched.

There was a soft tap on her door. She whirled and stared at it, her heart racing madly as she dashed the tears from her cheeks.

'Jessica?'

It was Sebastian, his voice sounding concerned.

'Are you all right?'

'Yes…yes, thank you,' she replied croakily.

'Evie feels very badly over what happened in the kitchen just now. And so do I. She's made you a pot of tea, and I have it here with me. Can I bring it in?'

Jessica groaned and fled to sit on the side of the bed. 'All right,' she called, hoping she looked like she'd just sat up.

He came in with a small tray, which held two mugs and a teapot, which meant he intended to join her. Everything inside Jessica tightened at the prospect, but it seemed an inevitability so she vowed not to make a fool of herself again with him.

Luckily, all the bedrooms in Lucy's Place were huge, each having a large writing desk and a chair over in a far corner. Sebastian headed for this to set the tray on, which meant he was a nice safe distance from Jessica.

'You have milk with no sugar, isn't that right?' he asked, glancing over his shoulder as he poured.

'You...you've got a good memory.'

'Unfortunately.' His remark was oddly rueful.

He smiled at her, but she couldn't smile back. She kept thinking he knew...knew about what he could make her feel, what he could make her want. Their eyes met, but once again, his thoughts remained hidden from her. She could only hope her face was as unreadable.

His smile turned slightly wry, and she stiffened. 'Evie was going to send you another slice of cake but I vetoed that. Did I guess correctly?'

'That cake could fuel rockets to the moon,' she retorted, and he laughed, the relaxed sound defusing some of Jessica's tension. He couldn't possibly laugh like that if he knew she was secretly lusting after him.

'It's a traditional Norfolk Island recipe,' he explained. 'Cooking here is a mixture of English and Polynesian. Things can be a bit stodgy occasionally, and bananas are a very common ingredient. We don't import fruit and vegetables, you see, and although we have shortages of other fruits sometimes, bananas are always in plentiful supply, particularly overripe ones.'

Jessica frowned. He sounded like he considered himself an islander. Did that mean he meant to stay on Norfolk Island indefinitely? 'Tell me, Sebastian, after this next month is over, and you've finished your book, do you intend going back to Sydney to live?'

'God, no.' He sounded genuinely appalled.

Jessica was taken aback. How could a man who'd been a high-flying dealer settle for such a quiet lifestyle?

'Never?' she questioned.

'Never,' he affirmed.

'You love it here that much?'

'I do, indeed.'

'Where will you live?'

'I'll find somewhere.'

'What will you live on?'

'I have enough.'

Which meant either her aunt had given him plenty, or that book advance had been a corker.

Another thought came to her, and having thought it, she simply had to ask. 'Do you have a lady friend on the island?'

Their eyes locked as he handed her her tea, and Jessica hoped hers were as bland as his. His coming close to her again was revitalising all those involuntary sexual responses he effortlessly evoked. Her breath quickened. Her blood began to race through her veins. Her face was in danger of flushing.

Only by a sheer effort of will did she prevent this humiliation.

'Do you mean lady friend or lover?' he asked rather coldly.

Jessica swallowed and tried to look as though she didn't care either way. 'Lover, I guess.'

'You seem rather preoccupied with my sex life. Without being rude, might I point out it's really none of your business who I've slept with in the past, or who I'm sleeping with at the moment.'

Now Jessica did flush. With a very fierce embarrassment. For he was quite right, of course. It was none of her business. But it was a subject dear to her heart—that treacherous heart that was thudding painfully in her chest within a body that was wanting him more and more with each passing second!

'I think I was entitled to ask if you were intimate with my aunt,' she said in heated defence of her own silly self.

'Why?'

'Because I—because… Well, if you'd genuinely loved and cared for her, I was going to give you some money,' she blurted, twisting the truth in order to get out of the corner she'd backed herself into. 'I felt badly about your being left out of her will.'

He stared at her for a long moment. 'That's very generous of you, Jessica,' he said coolly, 'but I wouldn't accept, anyway.'

'Why? Because you didn't genuinely love her?'

'Because I don't have any need of more money. I told you, money doesn't make a person happy.'

Jessica blinked at this turn of events. A genuine fortune-hunter would have jumped at her offer. Maybe he really wasn't interested in money. Maybe all he wanted was to live on the island and do nothing but write adventure stories.

'Besides,' he went on. 'That was not what Lucy wanted. The only reason I'm even still here, in her house, is to try to make her last wish come true.'

'And what *was* my aunt's last wish?'

'That you live here, of course.'

A very real resentment welled up in Jessica. If that was what her aunt had wanted, then she should have stayed that day. She should have given Jessica a chance to know her. She should have supplied her with some answers. 'I'm sorry,' she bit out, 'but I simply can't do what Lucy wanted.'

'You're still going to go back to Sydney at the end of the month, then?'

'I have to.' *Especially now…knowing Norfolk Island will always hold you, Sebastian Slade.*

'And you'll sell?'

'I can't see any other sensible alternative.'

His eyes hardened as they moved over her. 'So be it, then. I'll leave you now to your rest. See you at dinner.'

CHAPTER SEVEN

DINNER was served in the main dining room, Sebastian and Jessica facing each other across one end of the long lace-covered table, a bowl of red hibiscus blooms between them. Once again, Evie chose to eat in the kitchen by herself, saying she felt more comfortable that way.

The main course was delicious—crumbed fish, which needed no sauce to enhance its sweet flavour, a creamy potato dish with a hint of banana in it, and a fresh green salad. A chilled chablis from New Zealand complemented the flavours and helped soothe Jessica's agitation.

Unfortunately, Sebastian had presented himself for dinner in scandalously tight blue jeans and a chest-hugging white T-shirt, both of which did nothing for her renewed resolve to try to ignore her unwanted feelings for him. She had discarded her white cheesecloth outfit in favour of a modest and very opaque pants-suit in pale green silk, though she had showered at length, shampooing the humidity from her hair, then blow-drying it thoroughly before leaving it down.

Sebastian was wearing a bright red bandanna high around his hair, probably to keep it from falling into his food when he bent forward. Jessica couldn't help but admire once again the natural wave in his hair, not to mention its glorious colour.

Hers was plain black and dead straight. Its only plus

was its thickness. She still had to spend a small fortune having its bulk regularly thinned then expertly cut so that it fell in a stylish curtain to her shoulders when down.

'You're staring at me,' Sebastian commented quietly, then lifted his glass to sip his wine and stare at her over the rim of the glass.

Pride demanded she not look away or blush with mortification.

She managed the former very well, and she hoped the dim light masked the latter.

'I was admiring your hair,' she confessed with a blunt ruefulness. 'Most women would give their eyeteeth for it.'

'Really?' he drawled. 'I was admiring your outfit. Just how many did you bring?'

'There's nothing about me you admire, Sebastian. You think I'm a hard-hearted, money-minded, insensitive bitch. Why not admit it?'

He laughed. It was a harsh, caustic sound. 'Am I so transparent?'

'You've made it perfectly obvious what you think of me.'

'As you have of me,' he countered smoothly. 'Which is a pity, really. I'm sure Lucy hoped we'd like each other.'

'And why would that be?'

'So that I could more easily persuade you to stay on here, of course. That's why Lucy put that condition in her will. She knew there would be no more convincing salesman for a cause than a convert.'

'She'll have to be disappointed then, won't she?'

'So you're still determined to sell? You won't even consider a compromise?'

'Such as what?'

'Such as keeping the house as a holiday home and visiting here occasionally. Maybe, in time, you'll get to love it so much you wouldn't want to go back. I could look after the place for you, if you'd like. Earlier, you offered me money. Offer me a house-sitting job, instead. I'll take that.'

He didn't understand, of course. It was his presence in the house that would keep her away, not any imagined dislike of the island.

'I'm sorry, Sebastian,' she said, 'but I find the idea of keeping a home this size for me to holiday in only four weeks a year totally impractical. I would prefer to lease it to someone to run as a guesthouse. Or pay someone to run it for me. Would you be interested in doing that?'

She could handle him from a distance, and on the end of a telephone. Just.

'No, I would not,' he snapped. 'That's not what Lucy wanted. She wanted *you*—her flesh and blood—living here and loving it as much as she did.'

'That's a very romantic notion.'

'Lucy *was* a romantic. Not like some other women I've known.' This with a meaningful glance Jessica's way.

She bristled and was about to bite when she decided not to give him that satisfaction.

'If Aunt Lucy wanted me to live in this house so much,' she pointed out, 'then she should have stayed that day in Sydney. She should have let me get to know her. And she should have explained what happened between her and my mother. I'm not at all sure I could ever live happily in this house not knowing what happened here. And now I'll never know, will I?'

Sebastian pursed his lips, then took a thoughtful sip of his wine. 'Did you ask Evie?'

'Yes, and she has no idea what was behind their falling out.'

'Well, if Evie doesn't know, then I can't imagine anyone else on the island knowing, either,' he muttered.

'That's what I thought. Unless Aunt Lucy told *you*, of course,' she said, locking eyes with him. 'Did she, Sebastian?'

'No,' he denied firmly. 'She did not.'

Jessica let out an exasperated sigh. 'I can't believe she didn't tell anyone. Or leave some clues to the truth.'

Sebastian said nothing, merely put the wineglass to his lips again and swallowed more deeply. There was something wearily dismissive about his gesture, as though he was already very tired of her and would be glad to see the back of her and her questions.

She felt personally rejected and perversely piqued. So much for her resolve to ignore her feelings for him.

'I know you'd like nothing better than for me to shut up about all this,' she snapped. 'But I have no intention of doing so. What peeves me most is why you all jump to the conclusion that Aunt Lucy was the injured innocent, yet she was the *older* sister. Maybe my mother was the wronged party. Maybe Aunt Lucy left everything to me out of guilt!'

Sebastian's right eyebrow lifted in a surprised arch. 'It's a remote possibility, I suppose. Though if you'd known Lucy personally, you'd know there wasn't a nasty bone in her body. Isn't that right, Evie?' he said as Evie bustled in.

'What's right?'

'Lucy would never have deliberately hurt a fly, would she?'

'Oh, no. She was a very gentle, good-hearted woman. I never knew her to tell a lie in her life, or to speak badly of anyone. She always believed the best of people. The only time I ever saw her really angry was on the one occasion when she was confronted with absolute proof of someone's wickedness and barefaced lies.'

Evie continued talking as she gathered their dirty plates. 'There was this girl whom Lucy used to employ to do the laundry. Her name was Marie. One day, a guest's blouse—a beautiful blue silk thing—went missing. The guest claimed she'd put it out to be washed and ironed, but Marie vowed she'd never seen it, let alone washed and ironed it.

'Three months later, after the guest had long gone, Lucy and I dropped in to the worker's club for morning tea and there was Marie, wearing the blue silk blouse. My God, you should have seen Lucy. I've never seen her so angry. She made sure everyone on the island knew the girl was a no-good thief, so much so that Marie had to go to the mainland because no one here would give her work.'

'Maybe that's what my mother did,' Jessica mused. 'Maybe she stole something, and Lucy found out about it and banished her.'

'Seems a bit harsh,' Sebastian put in.

'Certainly does,' Evie agreed. 'Joanne was family, and Lucy was big on family.'

'Yet she didn't have a family herself,' Jessica commented.

'It seemed she couldn't, the poor love,' Evie informed them. 'She was right cut up about it. Bill, her husband, didn't seem to mind so much. There again, he wouldn't have made much of a father. He was a man's man, always out playing golf and going fishing and the like. It was the fishing that did him in, in the end. He was washed overboard during a storm. Lucy was inconsolable for a long time. I don't mind saying it was me who got her on her feet. I gave her the idea of running this place as a guesthouse. Said I'd help her with the cooking and such. She perked up no end once there were people in the house. She always was good with people.'

Except her own sister and niece, Jessica thought ruefully.

'You're right there, Evie,' Sebastian agreed. 'I think Lucy's greatest virtue was her ability to lend a sympathetic ear.'

Jessica said nothing, but privately she was getting heartily sick of feeling guilty just because she wasn't falling in with her aunt's last and probably guilt-ridden wishes. Jessica believed that no matter what her mother had done, her sister should have come after her much sooner. My God, she'd waited nearly thirty years! She wouldn't have come then, either, if she hadn't been dying.

No, Jessica felt no deep obligation to fall in with her aunt's wishes. Her only regret was that she could not lift the whole of this lovely house and transfer it to a beachside suburb in Sydney. She would have liked nothing better than to live in it and look after it, but not on Norfolk Island, and nowhere near Sebastian Slade.

'Both of you are having dessert, aren't you?' Evie asked.

Jessica thought of the banana cake and her figure. 'Er...'

'We definitely are,' Sebastian overrode her, bringing a sharp glance from Jessica.

'Worried about running to fat, city girl?' he taunted once they were alone. 'Won't your lover love you any more, if you deviate from your perfect size eight?'

'I don't have a lover,' she snapped. 'At the moment.'

'Poor Jess. Is that why you're so tetchy?'

Jessica had had enough. 'What is it with you? Why do you keep needling me like this? What have I ever done to *you*?'

'You were born,' came the bald and decidedly bitter-sounding announcement.

'Meaning if I hadn't been, you'd have inherited all this yourself?'

'Not at all. Meaning if you hadn't been, I might have been able to finish my book on time.'

'I won't stop you. I didn't ask you to take me sight-seeing tomorrow. I can get a map and take myself sight-seeing. I don't need you to do anything for me.'

'I realise that, dear Jess, but you wouldn't want me to break a deathbed promise, would you?'

Evie arrived at that moment with dessert, a huge helping of sherry trifle and jelly and cream.

She tutted as she placed their plates in front of them. 'I could hear you two out in the hall, bickering away like naughty children. I won't come cook for either of you if you don't start behaving yourselves. You *are* going to let Sebastian take you sight-seeing, my girl,' she said sternly to Jessica. 'And you're going to be very nice about it, aren't you, Sebastian?' She folded her arms and glared at him.

'You've shamed me into it,' he said dryly.

'I sincerely hope so.' Her hands moved to her hips. 'Now smile at her, me lad, and use some of that charm of yours to sell her this place and Norfolk Island. That's what Lucy wanted you to do, wasn't it? Why else would she have arranged for you to be here during Jessica's stay?'

'Why else, indeed?' he muttered.

Evie rolled her eyes and left the room.

Jessica went to say something, but her words died when those incredible blue eyes of his fastened onto hers. He lifted his wineglass in a toast, his mouth pulling into the most appallingly sensual smile.

It electrified every nerve ending she owned, tugged at her heart and turned over her stomach.

'To my new-found charm and your unlikely conversion,' he mocked softly.

Jessica was proud of herself when she scraped up a cool smile in return. She even raised her glass in a counter toast. 'You've got a snowball's chance in hell, Sebastian,' she said, not a quiver in her voice. 'But best of British luck to you.'

Jessica woke at three. Exhaustion had sent her to bed straight after dinner, and she'd quickly fallen asleep. But now she was wide awake, and there would be no more sleep for her that night.

She lay in the huge four-poster bed meant for a couple and watched the lace curtains blowing beside the French doors. Sebastian had told her to leave them open to let in the cooling night breezes.

Sebastian...

He was there, in the bedroom next to hers. Only one wall away. Less than twenty feet.

So near and yet so far.

Jessica groaned softly into her pillows. Why did she want him so much? It was perverse in the extreme when it was obvious he didn't even like her, let alone want her in any way, shape or form.

Could that be part of the reason? Was she challenged by his indifference? Jessica had to admit she wasn't used to men being indifferent to her. Even the ones who hadn't liked her professionally had found her physically attractive.

Sebastian, however, seemed immune to her looks. Or was it career women he was immune to? There was no doubt he was scornful of her ambition and drive. Scornful of her unwillingness to throw in her life in Sydney and move here to live.

Yet that was so unfair! Why should she abandon everything she'd worked for because an aunt she didn't know wanted her to? And why should she adopt a life-style that would not come naturally to her? It was all very well for Aunt Lucy to leave her everything now, then try to manipulate her from the grave, but where had she been when Jessica had really needed her, when her mother had needed her?

No. Aunt Lucy had a lot to answer for, in Jessica's opinion. If she'd been the wronged party in the feud between the two sisters, then why hadn't she told someone about it? Why keep silent?

'Because she was probably the guilty party, that's why,' Jessica muttered. 'She left me everything out of guilt!'

A creaking floorboard outside her door stopped Jessica's heart in its tracks. As she lay there, deathly still, her instantly alert ears made out the soft footfall of someone walking down the hallway. The sound of a door opening and shutting was more distinct.

Eventually, Jessica let out her long-held breath, though her heart was still racing. It seemed Sebastian was having trouble sleeping, too. Or hadn't he gone to bed yet? There was a dull light on the veranda, which she'd thought was moonlight, but which she now realised was coming from his room. Maybe he'd stayed up late, writing.

More sounds filtered through the door. Sebastian moving around somewhere, possibly in the living room across the hallway. What was he doing? Getting a book to read? Pouring himself a nightcap, perhaps? She'd noticed earlier that that room contained quite a library, plus a large rosewood sideboard with decanters full of whisky and sherry and port sitting in a row on lace doilies.

The thought of Sebastian awake and prowling around the house gradually began to unnerve Jessica. What was he doing? What was he wearing? Why didn't he go back to bed, damn it?

Time passed. Three-thirty came and went, then four. Finally, Sebastian returned to his room and switched off his light. She heard the squish of his mattress as he climbed into bed. Soon, the house was deathly silent.

Jessica couldn't go back to sleep. She lay there, thinking thoughts that unnerved her even more. She was becoming obsessed with the man, she realised. Totally obsessed.

Tomorrow was going to be a nightmare!

CHAPTER EIGHT

'IT's beautiful, isn't it?' Sebastian said as he pulled the Mazda to a stop and cut the engine. They were less than a minute from Lucy's Place, halfway down the steep hill she had seen from the back veranda.

What she hadn't been able to see from the back veranda, however, was this magnificent view of the foreshore below, not to mention the collection of impressive Georgian buildings at the base of the hill.

'Captain Cook described the whole island as paradise when he first saw it,' Sebastian informed her, 'but this part is my favourite. That's Kingston down there, where the British first settled and built the convict gaol early last century. The gaol is in ruins now but the government buildings are all still in use. They're well worth a look, inside as well as out.'

'Not this morning, though,' Jessica vetoed, thinking that would take hours. And she didn't want to be with Sebastian for hours. Their brief moments at breakfast together had been trial enough.

Jessica had risen around seven, showered and dressed sensibly in fawn Bermuda shorts with a striped fawn and cream shirt, which was slightly baggy, revealing nothing of her figure. She'd wound her hair into a tight knot and applied no makeup except a coral-coloured lipstick and some mascara, emerging from the bathroom looking cool and composed while inside her stomach was a mass of butterflies.

Silence from Sebastian's room had assured her she'd be able to breakfast in peace, and she'd almost managed it, too. But he'd appeared as she lingered over a second cup of coffee, looking slightly bedraggled but appallingly sexy in black satin boxer shorts and nothing else.

Jessica had fled the room as quickly as politeness allowed, but there was no fleeing now, ensconced as they were in the small Mazda.

Thank goodness he'd put on a T-shirt to go with the white shorts he was wearing today. At least she could look at him and not want to touch him so much. But it was still difficult to sit so closely to him in a car and not be brutally aware of every living, breathing pore in his beautiful body.

'Why not this morning?' Sebastian asked.

'First, I really need to go to the bank before lunch,' she said, thinking up any excuse she could to shorten her torture. 'And I have a couple of personal items I simply *have* to buy. There's no rush for me to see everything this morning, is there? I can drive myself down here any time now that I know the way. It's not far.'

'It's not the same on your own,' he said. 'You need a proper guided tour. There's always this afternoon, I suppose.'

'Oh, no, you don't. You said you write every afternoon. Can't have you accusing me of holding up your writing, can I?' she finished, throwing him a false but very bright smile.

His laugh surprised her, for it had an odd note to it, as though she'd made a sick joke. 'I'll just give you a quick drive-by tour of the major points of interest, then. After all, we can't risk you actually soaking up any of the atmosphere of the place. You might find you like it, and then what would you do?'

Jessica declined to answer his sarcastic question because he didn't expect her to. But she did deliver a droll glance his way then turned to look through her window while he reengaged the engine and drove slowly down the hill.

After being whisked around Sydney a lot in taxis, it felt to Jessica as though they were crawling. When Sebastian slowed down to snail speed at the bottom of the hill, she sighed in exasperation. This was his idea of quick? At this rate their drive-by tour would take hours, as well.

'I thought you were allowed to do fifty around the island,' she pointed out tartly. 'Are you trying to annoy me on purpose?'

'Heaven forbid I'd do such a thing, or delay the time it will take to satisfy Evie that I've done the right thing by Lucy's wishes. Unfortunately, the speed limit through the town and down here in Kingston is only twenty-five. Didn't they tell you that when you arrived? Drivers also have to give way to all livestock,' he added when he pulled up abruptly.

One of the cows grazing on the common had done an unexpected right turn onto the road, followed by a flock of geese.

'Or are you so desperate to vacate my company that you would rather I ignore the rules and run them down?' he added.

Jessica decided enough was enough. Things were getting out of hand. She had two courses of action. She could return sarcasm for sarcasm, whereby the month ahead would quickly deteriorate from one of secret sexual frustration to a very nasty episode indeed. Or she could attempt to defuse the growing antagonism between them, thereby making the situation tolerable, at least.

Common sense and her own survival demanded the latter solution.

'Wherever did you get the idea I was desperate to vacate your company?' she asked lightly as they waited for the geese to complete their casual trek across the road.

'Oh, come now. Let's not pretend.'

'In the interest of civility and politeness, Sebastian, *let's*,' she said firmly. 'I understand your disappointment that Lucy's last wishes are not going to be fulfilled exactly as she planned. I fully understand I am everything you deplore in a woman. But let me assure you that—'

'That's not true,' he broke in brusquely, moving ahead slowly now that the road was clear. 'At least, that last bit you said isn't totally true.'

'Oh, come now,' Jessica drawled, echoing his earlier sarcasm. 'Let's not pretend.'

His laughter carried real amusement, as did his sidewards glance. 'Very well. I confess. Underneath, I deplore you. Or at least, the type of woman you project sometimes. But in the interests of civility and politeness, and Evie's possible punishment, I'm willing to pretend if you are.'

'Done!' she said, experiencing a weird stab of pleasure when he smiled at her. It had to be a sexual thing, she supposed, yet it didn't feel sexual. It was as though their secret conspiracy to feign friendship had sparked the beginnings of a very *real* friendship. For the first time since they'd met, they had agreed on something, and it felt surprisingly good.

She smiled at him.

Unfortunately, it had the opposite effect to the one she was looking for. His smile immediately faded, his eyes glittering with that old hostility. 'Don't pretend too well, Jess,' he said curtly. 'We don't want to give Evie false hopes, do we?'

'False hopes?'

'She's one of those romantic souls you despise. Smile at me like that too much and she might start thinking you've fallen in love with me, and Lord knows what complications that would bring.'

Jessica stiffened, her heart going cold under his rebuke. God, but he was a right bastard. She wished she hated his body as much as she hated his spitefully nasty tongue. And he called *her* cynical!

'Don't worry,' she retorted, pique firing her tongue. 'I don't think Evie will ever be under the misapprehension I've fallen in love with *you*, Sebastian. As much as you deplore my type of woman, I deplore your type of man. I like my men smooth and smart and sophisticated, both in their appearance and their lifestyle. I like them with ambition in their hearts, fire in their belly and passion in their eyes. For *me!*'

Jessica might have tossed her hair over her shoulder at that point, if it hadn't been slicked into a tightly controlled knot. Instead, she lifted her nose and chin in a disdainful gesture. 'I don't go for drop-outs who slop around in next to nothing, whose hair looks like it hasn't seen a barber in years, who think working for a living is dabbling at writing between labouring jobs. I especially don't like men who look at me like I was something nasty that had just crawled out from under a stone.'

Her tirade over, an electric silence fell on the car as it moved slowly across a small stone bridge then through a narrow wooden gateway. The ruins of the gaol squatted on their left—massive, bleak-looking stone walls behind which lay God knew what.

Not much, she realised when she peeked through an archway. It looked like everything inside had been stripped and largely levelled.

The outward shell of a smaller houselike building stood on a rise to their right, broken stone steps leading up to a gaping and empty doorway. A large stone monument of some sort stood in the middle of a sweep of lawn in front of them. Behind it were more old buildings, some in ruins and some not. The bay lay just beyond, a long concrete pier jutting out into the rough water.

'Have you finished?' he said coldly as he swung the car to the left and towards the gaol.

'Quite.'

'Good, then shut up and listen.'

She thought he was going to tear strips off her. Instead, he began a monotone commentary about the history of the gaol and the surrounding buildings.

Jessica didn't hear any of it. All she heard were her inner churnings. *What on earth possessed you to say all that, you idiot? He'll really hate you now. He'll certainly never look at you as you want him to look at you, with passion in his eyes.*

'Are you listening to me, damn it?' he suddenly snarled, and she jumped in her seat, the startled blankness in her face revealing her inattention to the history lesson.

He swore and accelerated down the narrow tarred road, the car jolting over a hump, which proved to be an ancient convict-built bridge.

'That's the old salt mill on the right,' he snapped, indicating a towerlike structure amidst some isolated pines on a grassy point. 'And this is Emily Bay.'

The road ran around the edge of the bay, with a thick forest of Norfolk pines behind it. Jessica lost sight of the water for a while till the car emerged on the other side on a bare rocky point, which boasted one rather straggly pine but a spectacular view.

Sebastian parked, facing towards Emily Bay, apparently to allow his passenger a few minutes to soak in the postcard scene. Or maybe to regain control of his temper. Jessica wisely decided not to ask which. She stared silently through the windscreen at the bay, searching for something to say.

Jessica's idea of beach heaven was Bondi, at home, with its high surfboard-riding waves and people-pounding promenade. She even liked the wall-to-wall bodies on the beach on hot summer days. Of course she didn't go there to swim. She went to feel the throb of life around her, to keep that awful feeling of loneliness at bay.

So when she looked at the small reef-protected cove with its calm blue-green waters, one single swimmer and an almost deserted sweep of sand, she could appreciate its quiet beauty, but not the sense of solitude it evoked. When she looked at it, she thought loneliness, not peace. Boredom, not relaxation.

But she knew to say as much would bring more scorn from Sebastian's lips.

'It's very beautiful,' she said at last.

She could feel his eyes upon her but refused to look over and see his scepticism.

'Do you like to swim?' he said. 'I come down here for a swim most nights during the week before dinner. It's usually deserted by then. You can come with me, if you like.'

The idea both terrified and fascinated her. To swim in that secluded cove in that warm-looking water with a near-naked Sebastian every evening. The scenario evoked erotic thoughts in her head and a fierce longing in her body.

'You don't have to take your pretence that far, Sebastian,' she said stiffly.

'Evie will suggest it,' he retorted. 'I was just getting in first. It's a large enough area. You don't have to swim anywhere near me.'

'All right, then,' she agreed tersely while thinking she was insane. What was she trying to do to herself? 'Now, do you think we might go up to the shopping centre and the bank?'

'No more sight-seeing this morning?'

'Not today. We don't have to do everything in one day, surely. I'm going to be here a whole month.'

'You could be here a year, Jess, and I doubt we'd do everything,' he said dryly.

Jessica suspected she'd just heard a snide double entendre, but she treated his words at face value. 'I had no idea Norfolk Island offered such a variety of entertainment.'

His expression remained bland, though the corner of his mouth twitched a little. 'I'm sure you didn't. Perhaps I'll be able to surprise you.'

'I'll look forward to it.'

He looked at her and laughed. 'I have to admire your capacity for pretence, Jess. I only hope I'll be able to keep up with you. So what are these personal items you are so desperate for?' he asked as he backed out of the parking spot and headed the way they'd come.

'Nail polish and remover,' she admitted, then cringed at how pathetic that sounded.

He glanced at her perfectly manicured and polished fingernails before lancing her with a questioning look.

'For my toenails,' she added. 'Their polish is chipped

and I didn't bring any red with me. I always wear red on my toes.'

'Chipped toenail polish,' he drawled. 'A true emergency, indeed.'

Jessica refused to let him niggle her, no matter what he said. 'So I don't like chipped toenail polish,' she answered lightly. 'Is there any real harm in that?'

'I guess not. To town then, and the shops. I might buy myself a decent hairbrush while I'm there. I do have one but most of the teeth are missing. Can't have you leaving me for dead in the grooming department, can I?'

'But what will Evie say,' Jessica mocked, 'if you come to lunch looking neat and tidy? She might think you'd fallen in love with me and are trying to impress me.'

'I don't much care what Evie thinks. You'll know the truth, Jess, and that's all that matters.'

'The truth?'

'That there isn't a chance in hell of my falling in love with you. You see, I don't like my women tough and hard and ambitious. I like them soft and sentimental and obliging. Most of all, I like them to like me. I'm funny that way.' He flashed her a patently false smile. 'But you can pretend, if you like.'

'Pretend what?'

'That you like me. You could even try soft and sentimental and obliging, for a change. And I could respond with pretend passion in my eyes. Evie would be delighted.'

Suddenly, Jessica felt like she wanted to cry. Couldn't he see she wasn't cold or hard at all? If she was, he wouldn't be able to hurt her like this with his cruel barbs.

'I'm not much of a one for pretending,' she said thickly. 'So just shut up and drive me to town. I'm suddenly very bored with this conversation and with this tour.'

'Oh, well, I wouldn't want to bore you.'

He sped up the hill, doing more than fifty, she noted ruefully. But wild horses wouldn't have dragged a remark from her. Or a protest.

Shopping was swift and silent. Lunch was swift and silent. The afternoon was not swift, nor silent.

'I hate him,' Jessica muttered as she paced noisily around her room. 'Hate him. Hate him. Hate him.'

'For pity's sake will you shut up in there?' Sebastian called through the walls. 'I can't concentrate with you prowling around like a caged lion, mumbling away to yourself. Go for a drive or something, will you? Just be back in time for us to go for our swim.'

Jessica stalked onto the veranda and along to his room. She stood in the doorway, hands on hips, glaring at him. The trouble was she was glaring at his back. He was seated at the writing desk in the corner, tapping away on the keyboard of a small PC. 'I don't know if you've noticed,' she snapped, 'but it's begun to rain.'

'So?' He swivelled round from his PC to look at her.

'I don't want to drive around into the rain. I also won't want to go swimming in the rain.'

'Why not? The water's lovely and warm when it rains.'

'To be honest, Sebastian, I don't much enjoy swimming.'

'Why not?'

'I'm not very good at it.'

'Practice makes perfect. Besides, you've nothing else to do except paint your nails.'

'Thank you for reminding me. That should take me all of ten minutes.'

'You could weed the garden, if you like.'

'In the rain, with freshly painted nails?'

'It won't rain for long. It never does. It's stopping as I speak. As for the nails, leave them till last.'

She sighed. 'This is going to be a long month.'

'Amen to that,' he agreed, and turned to stare at the screen of his PC. 'Just go and do something, Jess. Anything. But do it quietly.'

Jessica glared at his steadfastly turned back, then whirled and stalked to her room. In the end, she did weed the garden, angrily at first, snatching the weeds out and swearing under her breath. But gradually, she began to quite enjoy the feeling of satisfaction that came with seeing each bed become clear of the offending and highly unattractive weeds. She couldn't do the whole garden in one afternoon, of course. So she set herself goals, deciding to do so much each day till it was done.

After she'd finished her goal for that day she took her slightly aching but much happier body inside, where she showered at length to get the kinks out of her legs and shoulders, then lay down for a small rest before doing her nails.

They never did get done, for she promptly fell asleep, not waking for a couple of hours.

'Where's Sebastian?' she asked when she emerged, yawning, to find Evie preparing dinner in the kitchen. The clock on the wall said five-thirty. The delicious smell from the oven indicated a roast dinner.

'He's gone for a swim. He said not to wake you.'

'Oh.' Jessica wasn't sure if she was disappointed or relieved.

'You know, I'm surprised you two haven't taken to each other more. Two smart good-looking people like yourselves. I would have thought you'd get on like a

Play the "LAS VEGAS" Game and get

3 FREE GIFTS!

FREE GIFTS!

FREE GIFTS!

1. Pull back all 3 tabs on the card at right. Then check the claim chart to see what we have for you — 2 FREE BOOKS and a gift — ALL YOURS! ALL FREE!

2. Send back this card and you'll receive brand-new Harlequin Presents® novels. These books have a cover price of $3.99 each in the U.S. and $4.50 each in Canada, but they are yours to keep absolutely free.

3. There's no catch. You're under no obligation to buy anything. We charg nothing — ZERO — for your first shipment. And you don't have to mak any minimum number of purchases — not even one!

4. The fact is thousands of readers enjoy receiving books by mail from the Harlequin Reader Service®. They like the convenience of home delivery... they like getting the best new novels BEFORE they're available in stores... and they love our discount prices!

5. We hope that after receiving your free books you'll want to remain a subscriber. But the choice is yours — to continue or cancel, any time at all! So why not take us up on our invitation, with no risk of any kind. You'll be glad you did!

Visit us online at
www.eHarlequin.com
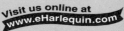

FREE!
No Obligation to Buy!
No Purchase Necessary!

Play the
"LAS VEGAS" Game

PEEL BACK HERE ▶
PEEL BACK HERE ▶
PEEL BACK HERE ▶

YES! I have pulled back the 3 tabs. Please send me all the free Harlequin Presents® books and the gift for which I qualify. I understand that I am under no obligation to purchase any books, as explained on the back and opposite page.

306 HDL C23K　　　　　　　　　　　　**106 HDL C2YS**

NAME　　　　　　　　　　(PLEASE PRINT CLEARLY)

ADDRESS

APT.#　　　　　　CITY

STATE/PROV.　　　　　　　　　　　　ZIP/POSTAL CODE

7 7 7 GET 2 FREE BOOKS & A FREE MYSTERY GIFT!

🍀🍀🍀 GET 2 FREE BOOKS!

🍒🍒🍒 GET 1 FREE BOOK!

🔔🔔🔔 TRY AGAIN!

Offer limited to one per household and not valid to current Harlequin Presents® subscribers. All orders subject to approval.

(H-P-05/00)

BUSINESS REPLY MAIL
FIRST-CLASS MAIL   PERMIT NO. 717   BUFFALO, NY

POSTAGE WILL BE PAID BY ADDRESSEE

HARLEQUIN READER SERVICE
3010 WALDEN AVE
PO BOX 1867
BUFFALO NY 14240-9952

NO POSTAGE
NECESSARY
IF MAILED
IN THE
UNITED STATES

house on fire. And I'd have thought Sebastian would be glad of your company, instead of avoiding it. He's been very lonely since Lucy's death.'

The thought of Sebastian being lonely, or missing her aunt, would never have occurred to Jessica. Yet it had occurred to Evie, who obviously knew Sebastian a lot better than she did, and had seen first-hand the nature of his relationship with Aunt Lucy.

Jessica could have kicked herself. There she'd been asking Evie all sorts of questions about her aunt and her mother, and she hadn't thought to ask her the one question she was dying to know the answer to.

'Tell me, Evie,' she began a little nervously. 'Were Lucy and Sebastian lovers?'

Evie shot her a startled look. 'Have you been listening to local gossip?'

'No. I just wondered. Has there been local gossip about them?'

'In a place as small as this? Yes, of course, there was. Heaps.'

'Well? *Were* they?'

Evie shrugged. 'I don't really know. If they were, they certainly hid it well. If you want my guess, I'd say not.'

'Wouldn't Lucy have told you?'

'Oh, no. Lucy and I were friends, but she never was one to confide personal details. Or even to gossip. Of course, there's always talk when a handsome young man is staying in the same house as a good-looking widow. And believe me, Lucy was a fine-looking woman when Sebastian first arrived. She looked many years younger than her age back then. It was the cancer that aged her.'

'I see,' Jessica said slowly, her disappointment acute. She'd been hoping Evie would clear up the matter one way or another. 'What do you think of Sebastian, Evie? Do you like him?'

'Yes, I do,' she said firmly. 'I didn't at first. But he's changed a lot over the past three years. For the better, I might add. He was very good to Lucy after she became ill. Very kind and caring. Nothing was too much trouble. Many's the time he sat with her all night when she was in pain. I can't speak too highly of him. I'm only sorry he hasn't chosen to show his good side to you. Perhaps he's upset that you're going to sell,' she finished with a reproachful glance.

Jessica didn't know what to think.

The sound of a car coming up the drive put paid to any thinking at all.

'That will be Sebastian now,' Evie said. 'You could always ask him yourself about his relationship with Lucy, you know? Though on second thought, perhaps not. He certainly hasn't taken to you, has he?'

Jessica had to laugh. 'You could say that.'

'Surprising. You're such a good-looking girl.'

'I'd better go freshen up for dinner,' Jessica said hurriedly when she heard the car door slam. The thought of Sebastian joining them in nothing but a wet swimming costume was unnerving in the extreme.

The white cheesecloth outfit made a reappearance for dinner, not because she was trying to attract Sebastian this time—difficult to attract a man who despised you—but because she didn't want him to make some sarcastic comment about her wearing a different outfit every day. She waffled over leaving her hair down and in the end put it up in a sleek French roll.

Sebastian presented himself at the dinner table wearing those appalling jeans again and a navy blue sleeveless

T-shirt which darkened his eyes to midnight blue in the dimly lit dining room. Another bandanna—navy this time—kept his hair out of his eyes.

He looked utterly gorgeous. It was impossible for her to keep her eyes off him. His opinion of her appearance was not similarly admiring, if the curl of his top lip was anything to go by as he sat down.

'I see you managed not to come swimming with me after all,' he remarked sourly. 'I'd prefer you to say you don't want to come rather than pretend to be asleep every afternoon.'

'Very well,' she said with a weary sigh when she realised he was going to keep the antagonism going between them. Jessica fell unhappily silent and began playing idly with her cutlery.

'What's wrong with you tonight?' he snapped abruptly. 'Are you sick, or something?'

Jessica's chin lifted, her jaw clenching. 'Not at all.'

It was a struggle from that point to keep the conversation from deteriorating into a sniping match, though to control her temper, Jessica drank most of the claret Evie served with the roast beef and Yorkshire pudding. She toyed with the thought of apologising to him for all the rotten things she'd thought about him, but in the end abandoned the idea. What was the point? Come the end of the month she would be gone from here, never to return. Sebastian would be a thing of the past, nothing but a bad memory.

'At least your sleep seems to have done your earlier mood some good,' he drawled over dessert—another fat-producing pudding complete with custard.

'I wasn't in a mood earlier,' she denied.

His eyebrows lifted. 'You mean you're usually like a cat on a hot tin roof?'

Jessica stared at him across the bowl of pink hibiscus. Was she so obvious? Surely he hadn't guessed he'd reduced her to a state of acute sexual frustration the like of which she'd never known before.

The cold gleam in his eyes gave him away. He was just trying to stir her. It came to Jessica then that whilst Sebastian might not be a callous fortune hunter, he was still a bit of a bastard.

'It might have escaped you, Sebastian,' she said shortly, 'but all this hasn't been easy for me.'

'Really? I haven't seen you suffering in any way.'

The bitter laugh escaped Jessica's lips before she could stop it. She'd never known such suffering, such torment. Even looking at him across the table had become torture, she wanted him so much.

Evie bustled in with coffee and after-dinner mints, bringing Jessica a welcome moment of distraction from her escalating blood pressure.

'I'm off now, folks,' Evie said. 'I've cleared up everything except what's on the table. Just pop your dirty plates in the dishwasher, and I'll finish up in the morning. There's a show on telly I want to watch, which starts at nine. See you tomorrow.'

'Bye, Evie,' they both chorused.

'I'm glad to see television isn't banned on the island altogether,' Jessica said dryly once they were alone. 'At least I can go over to Evie's in the evenings if my withdrawal symptoms get too bad.'

'I seem to be suffering from some withdrawal symptoms myself,' Sebastian muttered darkly. 'I wish a few hours of television would cure mine, but I very much doubt it. A few more days of this and I'll be ready for the funny farm.'

'What on earth *are* you talking about?' she said impatiently.

He arched a sardonic eyebrow at her as he downed the last of the wine. 'You mean you don't know? You *honestly* don't know?'

'No, I honestly don't know!'

'Then I'll just have to tell you, won't I?'

'That might be a good idea.'

His laugh was bitter. 'I doubt it. But the fact of the matter is this. I can't sleep and I can't write.'

Jessica blinked her bewilderment. 'Are you blaming *me* for that?'

'I'm not *blaming* you. But you *are* responsible.'

'Would you kindly like to explain that remark?'

'No, but having come this far, I might as well continue. The awful truth is that from the moment I set eyes on you yesterday, Miss Jessica Rawlins, I was madly attracted to you.'

'A-attracted to me?' she repeated dazedly.

'Well, actually, the word attracted is a bit of an understatement,' he said dryly. 'It was more a case of lust at first sight. Quite embarrassing, really. Surely you must have noticed me gawking at you like an adolescent schoolboy. Evie certainly did.'

So that was why he'd stared at her! But...

She swallowed as her fluster receded and the reality of the situation sank in. He wanted her as much as she wanted him. More, perhaps. He was a man, after all. She tried to speak but couldn't. She didn't know what to say.

'Yes, I can appreciate your surprise over my confession,' he drawled. 'I'm pretty surprised myself that I made it. But I'm just not good at pretending, like some people. Also, as you have no doubt noted, I've been behaving like an absolute bastard to you without sufficient

cause. Let me offer my sincerest apologies. My only excuse is that I have obviously been celibate far too long.
Now laugh if you like. It really is rather funny, isn't it?'

Jessica didn't laugh. She didn't find it funny in the
least! All she could do was stare speechlessly over the
table at the man she'd been wanting more than any man
she'd ever met.

'For pity's sake, Jessica, don't make me feel any worse
than I already do,' Sebastian snarled into the electric silence. 'I'm sure you're quite used to members of the
opposite sex being smitten by your striking beauty. Not
to mention your body. So stop playing the offended virgin. I really have no patience with it tonight. You and I
both know you're not that.'

She might have been angered by this last barb if she
hadn't been so shocked.

Having vented his spleen, Sebastian sat there, playing
with his empty wineglass, twirling it round and round. It
was unnerving to watch. Not that Jessica needed unnerving. She was already totally rattled by his astonishing
admission and the thoughts it evoked.

Now there was nothing standing between herself and
what she secretly wanted. He would not reject her. He
would welcome any admission or advance on her part
with open arms.

But it would only be sex on his part. And sex in its
most base form. He not only didn't love her, he didn't
even *like* her. He merely wanted to...

'What if I threw myself on your mercy?' he suggested,
his tone coldly self-mocking. 'Begged you to alleviate
my pain.'

'Pain?'

'Yes, pain. Do you have any idea what it feels like for

a man to want a woman so badly that it's a physical ache? Have you ever wanted anyone like that?'

'Yes,' she said. *You,* she thought bitterly.

'Then you know what it's like. Have some compassion, woman. Come to bed with me tonight. I'm a good lover. I won't disappoint you.'

She could not speak. Her heart was thudding too wildly, her blood pounding through her head. All she had to do was say yes and he would be hers. All that stood between herself and possible ecstasy was her pride and self-respect.

But pride and self-respect were important to Jessica. She had a feeling the reason her mother had ended up a drunken wreck was a lack of both at some point in her life. Jessica had never liked the concept of casual or selfish sex. That was for sluts. And men.

She'd been a virgin till she was twenty-two, and even after that, she'd always believed herself in love with the few men she'd allowed to bed her.

'But I don't love you!' she blurted, voicing her inner dismay that she was on the brink of blindly saying yes to him, despite everything.

His mouth twisted in a wry smile. 'I'm not asking you to love me, Jess, just to let me make love to you. I find it hard to believe that a woman as intelligent and sophisticated as you thinks sex and love always have to go together. Haven't you ever been to bed with a man you didn't love before?'

'No!' she denied hotly.

His astonishment was very real. His eyes flared wide, then narrowed. 'No?'

Her blush was so fierce it had to be visible, even in the subdued light. 'I...at least...not consciously. I thought I was in love with them at the time.'

'Hm. Interesting. And did they hurt you in the end? These men you thought you loved?'

'You could say that,' she said stiffly.

He nodded slowly. 'Love can be cruel. It demands too much, expects too highly. One is inevitably disappointed. Sex, however, never disappoints, if that's all one wants.'

'That's a matter of opinion,' she snapped before she could snatch the words back.

His eyes moved over her heated face—watchful, knowing and intelligent eyes. 'You've found sex disappointing, Jess?' he asked with a gentle curiosity that was incredibly disarming.

'Sometimes,' she muttered, looking into her untouched coffee.

'Sometimes, or always?' he persisted.

Her eyes jerked angrily to his. 'Will you just drop this?'

'No. I won't. I think it's a crying shame that a woman as beautiful as you has not had a satisfying sex life. It's also a mystery to me. You've no idea how much sensuality you project, Jess. It leaps from your body and your eyes all the time. That's why I have been like a cat on a hot tin roof ever since you arrived, because my poor frustrated male flesh was besieged by the silent messages sent out by your highly sexually charged self. Frankly I'm stunned to find out you're unfulfilled in that regard. I can only think you've been very unlucky with your choice of lovers so far.'

'And you think you'd do better? A man I don't love?'

'I'd sure as hell like to try,' he said, a wickedly sardonic smile pulling at his mouth.

'I'll just bet you would!' she flung at him.

She glared at him, at his mouth, his hands, his body. And she wanted them all. On her, and inside her.

His words came back to haunt her, those words he'd said to her that very first day, about how she could do what she liked out here on this island in this isolated house, and no one would ever know or judge. He was offering himself to her for the night, and she would be an utter fool to refuse. For it was what she wanted more than anything else in the world. If she let this chance go by she knew she would regret it for the rest of her life.

But it was so hard to say the words, to voice her agreement. Her tongue felt thick in her mouth, and the palms of her hands had gone clammy.

Speak up, her dark side urged recklessly. *He's yours. Take him!*

'All right then,' she said at last. 'Try!'

His smile faded abruptly, and he was very still for several excruciatingly long moments. 'You don't mean that,' he said at last, clearly sceptical. He hadn't expected her surrender, had not bargained on it.

'Oh, yes, I do!'

Heat flooded all through her body. *Now you've done it,* that dark little voice crowed inside.

But it was not met with self-disgust this time. Or shame.

A strange satisfaction rose to squash any negative feelings. There was a sense of triumph. And excitement.

Her chin lifted. 'I definitely do,' she repeated, her voice steady and strong and sure.

CHAPTER NINE

JESSICA stood on the back veranda, her hands curled tightly over the wooden railing, her shoulders squared against the feelings rampaging through her.

Delayed shock warred with a very real dismay at what she had agreed to in the dining room. Yet both kept being overridden by that voice, that dark and insidious voice that kept whispering wickedly weakening things inside her head.

You can't change your mind now. You don't really want to. You want him to take you to bed. You want him more than you've ever wanted anything in your whole life!

Jessica gulped down the gathering lump in her throat, then glanced at the clear night sky, with its full moon and myriad stars.

It was a night for lovers, she conceded. A night for romance.

But Sebastian wasn't looking for romance. Or love. He wanted what most men had wanted from her over the years, the difference being that this time, she wanted the same thing.

Sex.

Jessica shivered as she thought of all that small word entailed. The nakedness. The intimacy. The act itself. It was an extraordinary thought that soon she would lie beneath a totally nude Sebastian while he fused his flesh with hers.

It was less than forty-eight hours since they'd met. It felt like a lifetime!

As did the fifteen minutes since she'd agreed to give him her body to do with as he willed.

Oh, God, she thought despairingly. *What have I done?*

'What are you doing out here?'

She whirled to find Sebastian standing in the doorway, frowning at her.

'Have...have you finished?' she asked shakily. He'd offered to clear the table while she fled to the bathroom, instant nerves bringing on a sudden call of nature. She hadn't been able to bring herself to go to her bedroom and change into something more comfortable, as he'd suggested. Nothing was going to make her feel more comfortable at this moment.

'Yes,' he said, still eyeing her warily. 'The dishwasher is busily chugging away.'

'Thank you.' Jessica wrapped her arms around herself, feeling not cold but suddenly shy before him. Or was it ashamed? Did he think her cheap for having agreed to sex without love?

Probably, she accepted unhappily. That old double standard still applied, no matter how much women tried to change the status quo. A man who slept around without caring and commitment gained kudos from his mates, and was chased after by women for his prowess. He was a stud, whereas a woman of similar morals was a slut.

'I want you to know that I don't usually do things like this,' she said defensively, her arms still wrapped tightly around her.

He came forward and slowly but firmly unwound her arms before placing them around his neck. 'I can see that,' he said, sliding his arms around her then pulling her against him. 'It makes me want you all the more.'

He kissed her softly on her nose, then her cheek, then the corner of her mouth. Her lips were parted and quivering by the time he covered them with his own. There was no barrier to his tongue as it slid deep into her mouth.

Jessica linked her fingers behind Sebastian's neck and clung on like grim death lest she fall down, for her knees had suddenly gone to jelly and her head was spinning. His arms tightened around her, and she was dimly aware of her breasts pressed painfully against his chest.

Her main focus, however, was on that sensually probing tongue and how it was making her feel, what it was making her want. *Him,* inside her, not his tongue. Him, all over her. Him, and only him, for ever and ever.

She moaned a tortured denial at this crazy notion. Anyone would think she loved the man.

This isn't love, Jessica reminded herself brutally. *It's lust. Sebastian's a man of the world and he spelled it out to you earlier. You're enjoying sex without love, the same as men and wanton women have for centuries.*

Jessica shivered in his arms. Did that make her wanton? She certainly *felt* wanton under his plundering mouth and welded to his appallingly aroused body.

Vivid images flashed into her mind, starkly explicit and shockingly erotic. Sebastian, undressing her here, where they stood, touching her all over, taking her on this veranda, in the moonlight, her cries of ecstasy sounding shamefully loud in the stillness of the night.

'Jess,' he groaned thickly into her swollen lips.

'Mmmm?' The dazed murmur was all she could manage. She was still off in another world, a world where there was no shame, only the darkest and deepest of pleasures.

'You shouldn't have rubbed yourself against me like that,' he muttered. 'But no matter. It was probably all for the best. But I'll have to leave you for a minute or two.'

He was gone a full thirty seconds before she could assemble her jumbled brain enough to make sense of his words. When she realised what had happened, she groaned her embarrassment and spun round to grip the railing with a white-knuckled intensity.

Dear God, she hadn't even realised she *had* been rubbing against him. Though she accepted it must have been so. She'd been beside herself with longing for him.

Even now, with her fantasy fast fading, her heart was still pounding urgently within her chest. She wanted Sebastian back, with his mouth on hers again, and the hard warmth of his body enveloping hers.

As though her mind had conjured him up, he was suddenly there, his arms winding like steel bands around her chest from behind, pinning her upper arms to her sides.

'I was as quick as I could be,' he murmured as he nuzzled her neck, brushing cool lips across her burning skin. His arms were cool, as well, droplets of water on his fine body hair showing that he had showered during his brief desertion. 'I didn't want to waste all that lovely mad passion.'

Jessica only heard the word *mad*.

I must be, she thought dizzily. *Quite mad. He only has to touch me and I turn into a different woman. A stranger with totally alien responses and desires. Never before have I felt such abandon or excitement. He has totally bewitched me.*

'Tell me what you were thinking about earlier,' he murmured seductively. 'When I was kissing you.'

She shook her head, then gasped when his lips opened and closed on her neck, sucking at the already fevered skin till the sensations went from pleasure to pain.

'Stop,' she gasped, and wriggled against him.

It was then that she realised he was naked, totally, stunningly naked.

'Then tell me,' he insisted. 'I won't be shocked.'

Again, she shook her head, her eyes wide with the mental image of his nude body pressed up against hers.

'You were wanting me,' he whispered in her ear. 'Weren't you?'

'Yes,' she confessed with a shudder.

One of his arms released its hold to start stroking her throat, tipping her neck up and her head back against his shoulder with each upward caress. Her eyes squeezed shut when his hand moved down her throat, down to caress her cleavage, to tease and torment her as yet untouched breasts.

'*How* were you wanting me, Jess?' he demanded, his voice remaining soft and almost dreamlike. '*Where* were you wanting me?'

'Here,' she choked out, as though impelled to answer by his sheer willpower. 'Here,' she repeated, her voice becoming more dazed as his fingers continued to trace the curves of her bra.

'Here and now?'

'Yes,' she rasped.

'Tell me more. Tell me what I did in your mind.'

'You…you undressed me,' came her thickened words. 'And touched me.'

'Where?' His hand had slipped inside a bra cup, and one of his fingertips began gently rolling the rocklike nipple.

'E-everywhere.'

'And then what happened?' he asked, his voice amazingly calm, whereas hers, hers was trembling violently. 'Did I make love to you? Here, against the railing? As we're standing now?'

'Oh.' Her face flamed, along with her body.

'I see I did. And did I satisfy you in your mind?'

'Yes,' she groaned. Dear Lord, why didn't he stop making her talk about it? It was turning her on like crazy. His hand in her bra was turning her on like crazy. She felt like she was going to explode!

'How many times?'

She moaned her dismay. 'I...I don't know.'

'Has that ever happened to you before?'

She had to laugh.

His hand stilled on her breast. 'Are you saying you've never been satisfied by a man before?'

'Only...afterwards.'

'What about before?'

'Before?' Her tone echoed her bewilderment at the concept.

He removed his hand from her bra then, and slowly started to undo the buttons of her shirt while he kept her pinned against the railing, her back to him. Oddly, panic immediately assailed her, which was as confusing as it was disappointing. She hadn't felt panic in her fantasy. She had been all wild and willing abandonment.

But it seemed a fantasy was just that. A fantasy. Reality was not going to be as cooperative.

'No,' she said, her hands flying to cover his. 'I can't. Not out here.'

'Trust me, Jess,' he said, holding her hands still with one of his while he touched her with the other. His fingers moved with deceptive tenderness over her chest, reawakening her breasts through her clothes. Soon panic was the last thing on her mind. All she could think about was that warm, strong hand and where it was wandering. It moved up to stroke her throat and then her face, tracing her eyebrows and eyelids, her nose and finally her mouth.

She moaned as his fingers rubbed lightly over her lips. When they fell softly apart he inserted one of his fingers, and she found herself sucking on it, the mindless response echoing the fever pitch of arousal he'd brought her to, arousal that could no longer lay claim to conscience, or control, or command over what she was doing.

Her arms fell limply to her sides when he released them. She made no protest when he eased her away a little and finished undoing the buttons on her shirt. The thin white shirt was soon peeled back from her shoulders and discarded, along with her bra.

His hands on her bare breasts brought Jessica to some kind of awareness of what was going on, but by then she was so excited, so driven, she didn't care.

Maybe if he'd started being rough with her she might have snapped out of it. But he was all exquisite gentleness, his touch a tantalisingly tender torment. His hands cupped her breasts like they were spun gold, and he whispered to her his admiration of their beauty. He teased the nipples to an exquisite sensitivity, rotating his thumb pads over them in gentle circles, so unlike her previous lovers, who had been rough with her breasts in their impatience for their own pleasure, thereby giving her next to none.

There was such sweet magic in Sebastian's gentle hands as they adored her female shape. She moaned into the still night air under his soft caresses, groaning her dismay when he stopped.

But any dismay was quickly forgotten once he started

peeling her skirt and her undies down over her hips. Anticipation of what was to come held her spellbound as he pushed her clothes past her hips to fall to her feet.

'Oh,' she gasped when he wrapped one arm solidly around her waist and hoisted her off her feet so her panties fell from her ankles to the floor. He kept her aloft, bending his back—and hers—while his free hand smoothed down over her quiveringly tense stomach. She tensed when his fingers slid towards the damp curls between her legs, fearful that she would explode straight away if he even so much as touched her there. She'd never felt so excited in all her life.

And she didn't want to let go. Not yet. Please, not yet.

But he seemed to know exactly where to touch and where not to, to tease without giving her release. Closing her eyes, she leaned her head against his shoulder and wallowed in his expert foreplay. He balanced her on a razor's edge for what felt like ages before he abruptly changed tactics and touched her directly on that bursting bud of exquisite sensitivity.

'No!' she cried out. 'No, I...'

Too late. She was already splintering apart, her flesh contracting wildly. He lowered her swiftly, still gasping, onto decidedly unsteady feet, his hands steadying her around the hips while she grasped the railing for support. She knew what he was going to do—and oh, how she wanted him to do it! She was wanting him even more than she had before. Her legs moved restlessly apart, and she thrust backward as her desire searched to meet his.

She moaned as she felt him slide into her still throbbing body. She moaned again when her flesh gripped his with an intensity that was as foreign to her as it was fantastic. With a blind and suddenly wild urgency, she began rocking backwards and forwards.

'Oh!' she gasped, when astonishingly, she spilled into a second climax even more electric than the first, and far more satisfying. For she knew he'd be able to feel it and draw pleasure from it. She wanted him to feel pleasure in her, wanted him to join her.

Her back arched voluptuously and her bottom lifted to press hard against him, seeking to engulf him totally.

'God, Jess,' he muttered.

His hands moved from her hips, not so gentle now, grazing roughly over her painfully erect nipples as they swept down the front of her bowed body and up again. They roved hotly from breast to throat to her face again, in her mouth before stroking over her hair and down her back.

As she spun back down to earth, she began to sag beneath him, but he gripped her hard around her waist again, holding her up while he surged deeply into her.

Jessica was stunned when she slowly began to meet each powerful thrust, at first as though by some reluctant instinct, then more eagerly, till she was lost in sensation, lost to everything but the rhythm of his flesh within hers. She forgot time and place. Her eyes remained shut, and she was swirling in an erotic sea where pleasure didn't end. It just ebbed and flowed, not so intense now, but just as sweet.

At last she heard him cry out, felt him shudder within her. She sighed his name with a satisfaction as deep as it was dazed. Her legs went to jelly when he withdrew, and she might have collapsed if he hadn't swept her exhausted body into his arms.

'Sebastian,' she murmured again, looping her limp arms around his neck and pressing her face against the heavily beating pulse in his throat. She'd never felt so content, or so loved.

She was already half asleep when he placed her in the cool of his bed and pulled the sheet over her. But she knew she didn't want it to end yet, this feeling of oneness, of completion.

'Don't leave me,' she mumbled when his hands began to slide out from under her.

He climbed in beside her.

'Kiss me,' she whispered, her arms searching for his neck again.

He kissed her.

'Hold me.'

He held her and she sighed. He kept holding her and kissing her till she fell into a deep and dark oblivion.

Her last and very fleeting conscious thought was a stab of dismay that his loving attention was only an illusion. Sebastian didn't love her. He only lusted after her. Any attractive woman would have done. As he'd said, he'd been celibate too long....

Yet it was not of lust that Jessica dreamt in her sleep, but love. And it wasn't just any man loving her. It was Sebastian. They were married in her dream, married with a baby, married with many babies. There were babies all round her. Babies smiling. Babies gurgling. Babies. Babies. Babies.

CHAPTER TEN

JESSICA shot bolt upright in the bed, the word *babies* flying from her lips in a shocked gasp.

It took a couple of seconds for her eyes to focus in the darkened bedroom and see that the other side of the four-poster bed was empty.

A movement across the gloom beyond the bed drew Jessica's eyes to the large silhouette of a man filling the doorway that led to the moonlit veranda.

'Is that you, Sebastian?' came her panicky demand.

The figure came into the room, looming larger as it approached. 'Who else?' he drawled, and climbed into bed with her, giving Jessica a brief glimpse of a body as naked as her own. 'What is it? Bad dream wake you up?'

'In a way.' She lay back on the pillows and pulled the sheet modestly over her bare breasts, her embarrassment acute.

Talk about the morning after! Yet it was still the middle of the night.

She groaned when she thought of all she'd allowed and all she'd enjoyed. Then moaned when she thought of her dream.

'What's wrong?' he asked, levering himself on his elbow to stare at her.

Now that her eyes had grown accustomed to the light, she could see him quite clearly. His hair was no longer confined by the blue bandanna. It spilled in abandoned sensuality around his equally sensual face, bringing to mind all that he represented.

Nothing more than the pleasures of the flesh. There was no future with Sebastian. No hope of love, or commitment, or marriage. A baby by him would be a disaster! He might be the best lover in the world, but that would not make him a good father. He was thirty-eight years old, for pity's sake! If he'd wanted marriage and a family he would have had both by now.

'Sebastian,' she began, her voice betraying her panicky fear.

His brows drew together and he reached out to lay the most gentle hand on her cheek. 'What is it, Jess?'

'Did you...I mean...I couldn't tell...but did you... protect me?'

His hand fell from her cheek and his eyes grew cold. He dropped onto the pillows and linked his arms behind his head. 'Of course,' he said in a bored tone. 'Do you take me for a fool? But perhaps it was *me* I was protecting the most.'

His implication stung her to the quick. 'Come now, Sebastian. You might have been celibate lately, but Aunt Lucy wasn't always indisposed. And who's to say you were her first lover? She'd been a merry widow for some time, after all.'

He moved so fast she was flat on her back with her wrists pinned savagely to the bed before she could blink. 'Talk like that about Lucy again,' he said angrily, his mouth only an inch from hers, 'and I'll—I'll...'

His defence of her aunt's character sparked a dark resentment within Jessica. Plus a stabbing jealousy. Perhaps he'd really loved her Aunt Lucy, whereas all he felt for *her* was lust.

Well, at least he felt that, she thought wildly. At least

she could stir his senses…against his will, it seemed. He didn't like her but he'd wanted her, wanted her with a want that knew no pride. That was a heady thought, to have such power over a man.

Jessica savoured it, then acted on it. Without conscience or qualm.

Her tongue seemed to snake out of her mouth all by itself and sweep in an erotic circle around his lips.

'Or you'll what?' she taunted huskily, lifting her head to take his bottom lip between her teeth and nip it, not at all gently.

He wrenched his head back, releasing her so that he could wipe the back of his hand across his mouth. When he saw blood on his skin, he glared at her with a fierce gaze that made her tremble with a mixture of fear and excitement.

'You little bitch,' he snarled. 'I'll make you pay for that.'

'Promises, promises,' she returned, aware she was being provocative in the extreme but unable to stop herself. All she wanted was for him to want her again. She would do anything to achieve that end. Anything. 'Tell me what you like,' she said huskily, running her tongue over her slightly swollen and quite parched lips. 'Tell me, Sebastian, and I'll do it…'

He glared at her expectant and quivering flesh for a long moment, then abruptly rose from the bed and stalked out of the room, banging the door with shuddering force behind him.

Jessica lay there, wide-eyed and stunned. He wasn't going to make love to her ever again. That was how he was going to make her pay.

The thought brought despair to her heart, as well as her body. She could not bear to never again feel what she'd felt with him on that veranda. With a strangled sob, she leapt from the bed and went in search of him, vowing to say anything, do anything, to bring him back to bed with her. Her nakedness meant nothing to her as she ran from the room, calling to him.

She found him in the living room across the hallway, drinking a glassful of what looked like straight whisky. He hadn't turned on the light, but the large windows let in enough moonlight for her to see him quite clearly.

She gulped as her gaze abruptly encountered a full frontal view of his magnificent male body.

'So there you are,' she choked out from the doorway, and he slanted her a savage glance.

'Come to gloat, have you?'

'Gloat?'

He laughed and filled the glass anew from the whisky decanter on the sideboard. 'You played me for a sucker, Jess, and I, stupid fool that I was...I fell for it. Do you play these erotic games often? Does it turn you on to have each new lover think you've never been really satisfied before, thereby challenging them on to greater heights of passion? I should have known that a twenty-eight-year-old city girl who looks like you would have done it all by now.'

His tirade stopped just long enough for him to drain the glass with one long swallow.

'So what else turns you on?' he asked derisively as he whirled to fill the glass a third time, slopping some onto the lace runner. 'Believe me when I tell you I won't knock you back on any score. Let me get a bit more of this into myself and I'll be ripe and ready for anything. I just need to wipe that stupid idea from my head that what happened between us tonight was special.

'God, I must be going soft in the head! Maybe I *have*

been on Norfolk Island too long. I need a dose of Sydney
and some of its poisonously promiscuous women to get
me back on track. Fancy thinking I could mean something to you, when in reality I was just another one-night
stand!'

'No!' she denied hotly, tears welling up in her eyes.
'That's not true. Nothing you've said is true. I do not
have one-night stands, and you *are* special to me,
Sebastian. I've never experienced anything like what I
experienced with you tonight. Never! I don't know what
got into me just then. You…you seem to have released
something in me…something a little bit wild and wicked
and yes, wanton. But it's only for you, Sebastian. Only
for you…'

The tears were streaming down her face, dripping from
her nose and running into her mouth. She had never felt
as devastated as she had under his scorn. Or as despairing. His good opinion of her was suddenly more valued
than his lovemaking.

'Please believe me, Sebastian,' she said, sobbing. 'I'm
not what you think. I'm not.' Her head dropped into her
hands and she wept floods of tears.

His hands curving gently over her shaking shoulders
sent her sagging against him in relief and joy. 'You believe me,' she cried as she hugged him. 'You believe
me…'

He said nothing, however, and his lack of confirmation
finally sank in. Eventually, Jessica lifted her tear-stained
but dry-eyed face to his. 'You *do* believe me, don't you,
Sebastian?'

His expression was disturbingly implacable.

She pulled out of his arms. 'You *don't* believe me,'
she said, rather dazed.

'Does it matter? Tonight was a mistake. You and

I...we are a mistake. It won't work. Believe me when I say what happened tonight won't happen again.'

'You don't mean that!'

'I'm trying to,' he said, hard blue eyes raking over her nude body with rueful regard.

She saw his vulnerability and took bold advantage of it, moving to wind her arms around his neck and press herself against him. 'I won't let you go,' she said with all her natural stubbornness and new-found sexuality.

He held himself stiffly in her clinging embrace, but she could feel the effect she was having on him.

'What is it that you want of me, Jess?' he asked. 'Spell it out. And don't lie. I need to know the truth.'

'I...I want you to be my lover while I'm here,' she said truthfully. To want more was fantasy land.

'And when the month is over? What then?'

'What do you mean?'

'Will you be able to walk away from me and never look back? Never think of me or want me ever again?'

'I...I...'

'Swear to me now that you definitely won't fall in love with me!' he demanded fiercely, his hand grabbing her upper arms, his fingers digging into her flesh. 'That all you want from me is sex.'

She tried to say it. Her mouth actually opened, but she knew in her heart it would be a terrible lie. She was already half in love with him already.

'No,' she blurted, agonised by what she was admitting. 'I...I can't swear to that.'

A great shuddering sigh rushed from his lungs, and his bruising fingers gentled on her flesh. 'That's all right, then,' he said, and before she could blink, he swept her into his arms and kissed her.

'I've had my fill of hard bitches, Jess,' he told her. 'If

I'm to have a woman in my bed for the next month, then I want it to be a real woman, with a real woman's heart and feelings. God, for a minute there I thought you were going to so swear, and where would that have left me?'

He laughed, a sound mixed with self-mocking and delight. 'With a whole month of torment, that's where! Now…now I can make love to you as I want to make love to you, with no holding back, no reservations. Beautiful Jess,' he murmured, kissing her still startled mouth. 'Lovely Jess.' He kissed her again. 'Exquisite Jess.' And yet again.

Jessica was speechless as he carried her to his bed and laid her gently down. 'Tell me what you like, Jess,' he whispered. 'Tell me and I'll do it.'

Oh, God, she thought, and, sliding her shaking hands into his hair, she drew him down, first to her mouth, then to her breast.

He did her silent bidding, suckling at her erect nipple as though he were a hungry infant, greedy and demanding. Waves of pleasure flooded Jessica, tossing her this way and that. She moaned when he slid down her body to kiss and lick her stomach, then lower. Her legs seemed to open of their own accord, offering herself up to his lips with such trust she could hardly recognise herself.

And he did not betray that trust, showing her ecstasies she'd never known before. What fools her other lovers had been. What ignorant fools.

'No more,' she said at last with limp happiness.

He merely laughed and gathered her to him again, showing her that she still had no judgment over when her pleasure was done. He smiled triumphantly when his powerful possession made her feel that pleasure again, smiled and told her she was the most sensual, most beautiful, most wonderful woman in the world.

Jessica had never felt so happy. Or so tired. Sighing, she closed her eyes and was asleep in no time. If she dreamt, her dreams did not disturb her this time. She slept on and on, through the night and past the dawn. She might have slept till noon…if it hadn't been for Evie arriving to make lunch.

CHAPTER ELEVEN

'YOOHOO! Where is everyone? Anyone home?'

Jessica was instantly awake, recognition of the female voice hitting her simultaneously with the lateness of the hour. She wasn't sure exactly what time it was, but the sun was well up.

'Oh, my God,' she groaned. 'Evie!'

Sebastian's hand on her arm stopped her flight from the bed. 'She might as well know, Jess. There's no keeping it from her.'

Jessica stared at him as though he were mad, shrugged his hand off her arm and scrambled out of the bed. 'Don't you dare say a word,' she hissed, her heart beating madly. 'If you do, I'll kill you!'

He chuckled. 'If you do, it'll be Norfolk Island's first accredited murder.'

'Sebastian, don't joke,' she cried, embarrassment making her stomach curl. She could only imagine what Evie would think if she saw her with Sebastian like this, after they'd seemingly not even *liked* each other yesterday. 'Oh, my God, I just remembered my clothes. Will Evie see me if I creep out of here and round the back to my room via the veranda?' she whispered in desperation.

'Not if you're a quick creeper. She's sure to go into the kitchen first and make a cuppa. The kitchen window faces the front.'

'Thank God,' Jessica said with a ragged sigh.

'Aren't you going to kiss me before you go?' Sebastian said, smiling his amusement at her agitation.

'Don't be silly. Oh, all right.' But when she bent her mouth to his, he grabbed her and pulled her on top of him. She tried to smother her squeals as he tickled her mercilessly but feared she was very noisy in her struggles to free herself.

'I'll get you later,' she threatened as she pushed her hair from her face and stumbled across the room to the open doors. A warm breeze was wafting in, making her acutely aware of her nakedness.

'Promises, promises,' he drawled after her in a sardonic echo of what she'd said to him the previous night.

She didn't stop to spar with him this time, peeping up and down the veranda before running as quietly as she could around the corner.

The sight of her abandoned clothes brought her up with a jolt. They looked so…so *abandoned*!

Closing her mind to the memories that flooded in, she snatched them up and bolted to her room, expecting any moment to hear Evie's shocked voice behind her. But she made it inside without any humiliating encounters.

Her perfectly made and unslept-in bed seemed to stare at her, looking pure and pristine with its white lace quilt. Would she ever use it again during the next month? she wondered.

Not if I can help it, came the wicked thought.

No, not wicked, she denied. Wonderful. Being made love to properly was wonderful! She didn't aim to spoil it with any thought of blame or shame. She didn't know what the future would bring with Sebastian but she aimed to enjoy every single moment she had with him.

Let tomorrow worry about tomorrow! she decided with a recklessness new to her. She usually had a prosaic and pragmatic way of looking at life. She'd always been a planner, and so damned practical. To hell with that for the next month! To hell with everything except Sebastian.

Jessica carried a silly, fatuous smile into the shower with her. She was still carrying it when she made it to the kitchen some twenty minutes later.

'Well, if it isn't Miss Sleepyhead!' Evie said brightly from where she was chopping up vegetables at the sink. 'Sebastian told me he'd let you sleep in. He said he kept you up playing games till the wee small hours and that you were a bit wrecked. I had no idea you liked games. Lucy was quite an addict, too. Which one's your favourite?'

Jessica's whirling mind finally ground to a halt. She was going to kill Sebastian when she got him alone...amongst other things. 'Oh, I like them all,' she said swiftly, and tried desperately not to blush.

'That's good. It'll give you and Sebastian something to do in the evenings while you're here. You must be bored without a television. I must say your sleep-in seems to have done you good,' Evie rattled on. 'You look positively glowing this morning. Bright blue suits you, doesn't it?'

'What?' she said, distracted by her thoughts of the coming evenings. Boredom would no longer come into it, of that she was sure! 'Oh, yes. Blue. I suppose so, but I think blue looks good on just about anyone, don't you?'

Actually, she'd dragged on the blue shorts and matching singlet without much thought except for the heat. It was much warmer than it had been the previous day, the sun shining brightly. Her face was scrubbed free of makeup, and her hair was scooped up in a ponytail. She was a far cry from the sleek sophisticated number who'd stepped off the plane on Sunday, but she felt much more alive and incredibly relaxed.

'If you'd like a cuppa, I haven't long made a pot,' Evie offered. 'It should still be hot. You don't mind getting it yourself, do you?'

'Not at all,' Jessica said. She began humming as she did so.

'Pour Sebastian a mugful at the same time, will you?' Evie asked. 'He says he has a bit of a hangover this morning and hasn't been able to stomach any breakfast as yet. And I don't wonder why,' she added dryly. 'The whisky decanter's only half-full, I noticed. He said he had a touch of insomnia. Not that the drink seems to have done much good. You should have seen his bed. He must have tossed and turned all night. It was a right mess, with pillows on the floor and all.'

Jessica thought she did well not to look guilty, though she was relieved Evie's observations carried no noticeable insinuations. 'Insomnia's an awful thing,' she commented lightly as she poured the tea.

'I'll say,' Evie agreed. 'I'm making a simple grilled steak and salad for lunch, since Sebastian's stomach is feeling a bit fragile. Is that all right?'

'Perfect. I'll just take this tea along to him. Is he in his room?'

'Should be by now. He did pop along to the other bathroom for a shower and shave while you were showering. But I dare say he's back at his desk by now, writing away, trying to meet his deadline.'

He wasn't writing. He was standing on the veranda outside his room, dressed in nothing but shorts again.

Jessica swallowed as she walked through to join him, telling herself she would soon get used to his going around half-naked. Surely, she would not always look at him and feel an emptiness yawn in the pit of her stomach. Maybe, after he'd made love to her for a week or two, the intensity of her feelings would wear off.

'Here's the tea you wanted,' she said, smiling at him as she handed him the mug. She was glad that she'd thought to bring her own mug with her. It gave her an excuse to stay.

He gave her a strangely thoughtful look over the rim of the mug as he lifted it to his lips.

'What?' she asked.

'What what?'

'What are you thinking, silly?'

'That I'm going to be wicked and play hooky from my writing today.'

'Oh?' She was thrilled but tried not to show it. 'What happened to the hangover?'

'It's still there, hovering. But I can endure it provided I don't do any mental work. Not that I could. My creative ability seems to have still flown the coop. Actually, I'm feeling awfully basic this morning.'

'Hangovers *are* basic things,' she said.

'I wasn't thinking of the hangover,' he said dryly as his eyes washed over her. 'You could have worn a bra, Jess. What are you trying to do to me?'

She had to laugh. 'That's the pot calling the kettle black.'

'What on earth are you talking about?'

'Do you have any idea what *you* do to *me*, going around half-naked all the time? What you've done to me from the first moment I saw you?'

His eyebrows lifted, his expression going from surprise to a pleased speculation. 'No. What do I do?'

'You put indecent thoughts into my head.' And her eyes drifted over his bare chest and past his navel.

He groaned. 'God, don't look like at me like that, woman. It puts thoughts into places other than my head, and I'm just not capable of making love at the moment. Give me an hour or two.'

'Poor Sebastian.' She ran a teasing finger down the middle of his bare chest.

'I might have to have a little rest after lunch. Care to stroke my brow for me? And any other parts you fancy?'

'Only if I can brush your hair, as well.'

He seemed taken aback. 'Brush my hair? Why, is it that messy?' One hand reached up to rake through its tangled glory with an elegantly nonchalant grace.

'No,' she said. 'I just like the thought of brushing it.'

'Whatever you like.' He shrugged.

I'd like a lot of things, she thought as she looked at him and sipped her tea. *I'd like to touch you all over, kiss you all over. I'd like to massage sweet scented oils into your beautiful body and hear you groan with desire. I'd like to take you with me into the abyss you took me to last night, make you tremble and cry out with mindless joy.*

'Evie's making steak and salad for lunch,' she said, for all the world like lunch was the only thing on her mind.

He moaned. 'I can't think of food.'

'Don't think of it. Just eat it.'

He slanted her another of those thoughtful looks. 'You like giving orders, don't you?'

'No, but I'm disgustingly sensible.' *Most of the time,* she thought. 'Besides, someone has to give orders or nothing gets done.'

'Why should anything *have* to get done?' he said with a flash of irritation.

'Now don't start that with me, Sebastian. It won't

wash. You imagine you're a free spirit with your life here, but you still discipline yourself to write your book most days because if you don't, it won't get done.'

'That's different.'

'Why?'

'Because it's what I choose to do. No one orders me to do it.'

'How fortunate for you. Cast your mind back to when you were dirt poor and you'll find you didn't have that option. You had to work to live, and working usually involved someone giving and taking orders.'

'That's a smart mouth you have, Jess. Frankly, I'd prefer you to use it for other things than making me feel a fool.'

Her face flamed at the image of what he'd implied. He stared at her.

'Don't tell me you've never done that, either. That's stretching credulity too far.'

She looked away from his sceptical face, out at the view. 'Believe what you like,' she said, a painful constriction around her chest.

'Hey, don't get upset with me. I do believe you. Honest. It's just difficult getting used to your being so different to what I first thought.' He reached out to touch her face, stroking her cheek while everything inside her melted with longing for him. 'Not that I mind. I like the Jess I'm discovering.' The back of his hand grazed across her mouth. 'Such sexy lips, yet so innocent...'

They didn't feel at all innocent at that moment. They burnt to do all that his words evoked in her mind. Her eyes met his and she knew he saw her utter willingness to do anything for him. Sexually, anyway.

'Have you changed your mind yet?' he murmured, his hand drifting down to stroke her jawline.

'About what?' she asked, even though she knew what he was asking.

'About selling this place. I'll look after it free of charge...if it will keep you coming back to me.'

Despite her deciding earlier to throw caution to the winds, Jessica hesitated. 'No...I haven't changed my mind,' she said carefully. 'Look, let's not talk about that just now. If we do, we'll only end up arguing again, and I don't want to argue this morning.'

He snorted, then swept his mug of tea around in a panoramic wave. 'How can you possibly prefer the city to this?' he demanded.

Jessica looked at the deep valley, and while she saw its beauty and splendour, it was still just a view. See it every morning and you'd soon get used to it. 'It's very lovely,' she said. 'And I do appreciate it. It's very peaceful and relaxing.'

'Meaning it's a nice place to visit but you wouldn't want to live here,' he scoffed.

'I am not going to let you provoke me this morning, Sebastian. I'm too happy.'

He scowled for a moment, then smiled. It was a very sexy smile. 'What are you going to let me do, then?'

'Nothing you're not capable of, that's for sure,' she said, her eyes dancing with mischief as she lifted her mug of tea to her lips.

He took the mug out of her hands, balanced it with his on the top of the railing then drew her into his arms.

'I think this should wait till Evie leaves after lunch,' she said firmly. 'Much as *you* don't care if she finds out about us, I do!'

'Tough.' His kiss was as uncompromising as his attitude towards keeping their affair a secret.

'I thought you said you weren't capable,' she mocked

softly when his mouth finally lifted. There was nothing remotely incapable about what was pressing with undisguised urgency against her stomach.

He cupped the back of her head and kissed her again, quite savagely, his lips bruising as they reduced her supposed willpower to pulp. 'Now you know,' he muttered into her gasping lips.

She stared into wildly glittering blue eyes.

'Know what?' she whispered shakily.

'That I'm a liar.'

For a split second she didn't know what to think. There was something quite frightening in the way he was looking at her. But then he laughed, whirled her round and pushed her off with a smack on the bottom. 'Get thee behind me, Satan.'

Still slightly disoriented, she stopped and glanced over her shoulder at him, aware that she was suddenly holding her breath. But he was smiling at her so sweetly that her earlier momentary qualm seemed ridiculous. What possible reason would he have for lying to her? It wasn't as though he'd declared undying love, or proposed marriage, or anything like that. They were just having an affair. If Jessica secretly hoped for more than that, then it was her own silly female fault!

No, she had to stop hoping for too much and do what she'd vowed to do last night. Enjoy each moment for what it was and leave the future to fate.

With a surge of devil-may-care mischief, she whirled and walked towards Sebastian, enjoying the surprised flaring in his nostrils and eyes as she drew right up to him, her arms seemingly going round him in a tender embrace. When she drew back, laughing, with the empty mugs in her hand, his eyes narrowed and he pouted at her.

'I'm really going to make you pay for that one,' he warned darkly.

'Ooh. I'm petrified.'

'So you should be.'

'Before my punishment begins, would you be able to run me down to the shops again? I really must do my toenails this afternoon.'

'Let me guess. You bought the wrong colour nail polish?'

'No, I forgot the cotton wool balls. You have to separate your toes with cotton wool balls so that you don't smudge the polish.'

'How come I didn't think of that?' he scoffed.

'Because you're not a woman. As I said, I'm not going to bite today, Sebastian. Now, if you'd like to put a shirt on, we could get this little emergency fixed up before Evie serves lunch.'

'You're giving orders again.'

'You can punish me for it later,' she countered blithely, and swanned off to the kitchen before he could accuse her of wanting her bottom smacked, or some such other kinky thing.

'Sebastian's driving me down to the shops, Evie. We won't be long.'

'Better not be. Lunch in half an hour. Then I have to dash off. Monday's my craft afternoon. And I won't be back till five-thirty. What do you think you'll do all afternoon? You can bet Sebastian will get back to his book once he's got some food in his stomach.'

Jessica was amazed at her artfully nonchalant shrug. 'Oh, I don't know. I'm sure I'll find something to occupy my mind....'

CHAPTER TWELVE

'YOU two seem in bright spirits tonight,' Evie said as she served the evening meal.

Jessica swiftly forked some of the mouth-watering beef casserole into her mouth in an effort to hide her guilt from Evie. Though guilt was a bad word. She didn't believe she'd done anything *wrong* in spending all afternoon in bed with Sebastian. It had been a wonderful few hours, full of tenderness and pleasure, passion and fun.

Yes, fun!

Jessica smiled when she thought of Sebastian painting her toenails for her after she'd brushed his hair at length, then given him a long, deliciously sensual massage to get rid of the last vestiges of his hangover. He'd done an excellent job on her nails after a few practice runs, and while she'd giggled over his mistakes, it had been a surprisingly sensual experience, having a man paint her toenails.

Perhaps it had something to do with having him sit between her legs as she lay on the bed in spread-eagled nudity. Or the way his fingers kept brushing over the highly sensitive soles of her feet. By the time he'd finished, it had been hard to keep her bottom half still for five minutes while the polish dried. She'd wanted him so badly that she'd been easily seduced into accommodating him in more imaginative ways.

She'd never dreamt that her breasts could be used in

such a way. She couldn't claim to such an innocent mouth any more, either.

'Jess and I are great mates now, aren't we?' Sebastian said naughtily. 'I decided, in the end, to abandon my book for the day and do the right thing by our guest.'

'And high time, too, Sebastian. So, where did you take her? You had a lot to choose from since you only managed Kingston and Emily Bay yesterday.'

'Places the like of which she'd never been before.'

Jessica wanted to strangle him as an embarrassed heat started creeping up her neck and into her face.

'Well, of course she'd never been there before, you crazy man,' Evie pointed out impatiently. 'She's never been to Norfolk Island before, have you, Jessica?'

'No,' was all she could manage, averting her burning face while she picked up and ripped her bread roll asunder. She'd have liked to stuff it all into that mischievous mortifying mouth of his!

'Did you take her to Anson Bay?' Evie asked Sebastian.

'Not yet.'

'The top of Mount Pitt?'

'No.'

'Cascade Bay?'

'No.'

'Then where on earth *did* you take her?'

'I wanted to go to Kingston again,' Jessica lied in desperation to stop Evie jumping to the right conclusion. 'And I did some more shopping. Those duty-free prices are so tempting.'

'I promise I'll give her a more in-depth tour tomorrow, Evie.' Sebastian's glittering blue eyes were full of wicked promise as they locked onto Jessica's across the table. Dear God, just how more in-depth could her sexual education become!

She knew her cheeks had to be a fiery red by now, and this time, Evie noticed. Her eyes went from Jessica's face to Sebastian's before a decidedly wry smile appeared.

'I'm so glad to see you're getting along better than you were yesterday,' she said with deliberate understatement. 'Your Aunt Lucy would be pleased, I'm sure,' she said to Jessica.

Jessica bit her bottom lip as she realised she'd almost forgotten about Aunt Lucy, not to mention all those questions she'd been so eager to find answers to yesterday. Being in bed with Sebastian all afternoon had wiped everything from her mind but the present.

Now that she was reminded, her thoughts turned to her mother once more, and the mystery of her flight from her family and Norfolk Island.

'Speaking of Aunt Lucy, there's something I've been meaning to ask the both of you,' she said to Evie and Sebastian. 'Aunt Lucy must have left some personal papers and effects behind. Letters, photo albums and the like.'

Jessica frowned as she realised there were no photos around the house at all, either on the walls or sitting on shelves, which was unusual. 'Have they been packed away? I'd really like to look through them. There might be some clue to…you know…'

'There's a small boxful in the bottom of her wardrobe,' Sebastian said abruptly. 'She did throw quite a lot of things away when she knew she was dying, but you might find something in what's left. I doubt it, though.'

'Why's that?'

'I went through everything myself when I was looking

for her will. There's nothing relating to the falling-out Lucy had with your mother. Still, there are some photos you'd probably like to look at. I didn't think to give them to you. I'm sorry. It was remiss of me.'

She shook her head, knowing the blame was hers. 'I should have asked for them earlier. I don't know where my brains were.'

'There's no harm done,' Evie said kindly. 'You can look through them as soon as you've finished your tea.'

'I'll do that.' Already she was looking forward to doing so, hoping there might be something, *anything* to fill in those missing pieces.

'Don't go getting your hopes up,' Sebastian warned as soon as Evie left the room.

'I might see something you didn't,' she told him. 'A woman has a different perspective to a man.'

'True. Just don't go imagining things.'

'Such as what?'

He shrugged. 'God knows. Women have a capacity for complication and melodrama. They see problems where there are none. If there's only one simple and obvious answer to a question, they will still look for another. Alternatively, they would rather lie, to themselves and others, than accept an answer that is unpalatable to them.'

'I'm not like that. I'm a very clear and direct thinker. And I don't lie.'

'Want to put that to the test?'

'If you like.'

'How many lovers have you had before me?'

'Three.'

He was startled, but pleased. 'Three idiots, from what I can tell. You're well rid of them.'

'I fully agree, Sebastian. I much prefer you in my bed.'

'I hope you remember that when the end of the month comes.'

'I hope you do, too.'

His eyes narrowed on her. 'You think I'm going to come after you, don't you? I won't, you know. But I do want you, Jess. And not for just a miserable month. So be warned. When I want something I can be totally conscienceless.'

'I've been known to be pretty ruthless myself,' she countered blithely. 'So I suggest you reconsider your thoughts about living in Sydney, or at least visiting it more often.'

His eyes darkened to slate. 'God, but you're one stubborn woman!'

'So I've been told.'

'I won't play fair, you know.'

'This isn't a game, Sebastian. I don't play games with my life.'

'No. You're quite right. It's no game. It's deadly serious. You remember that.'

He glared at her, and she glimpsed a Sebastian she hadn't seen before. A ruthlessly determined Sebastian. The same Sebastian who'd once held a high-pressure job where only the bold and the brave survived for long.

Jessica quivered with a weird mixture of sexual arousal and fear. For she knew he meant to use her newly discovered sensuality against her. Use it quite mercilessly.

There was excitement in that idea. She would be a liar to deny it. He was so skilled at the art of lovemaking. And so much more experienced than she was. He could certainly take her to places where she'd never been before. Dark, alluring places.

But maybe some of them were places she should not

go. Surely there had to be danger in being so turned on that she lost all control!

'You…you wouldn't ever hurt me, would you, Sebastian?' she asked a little shakily.

Shock sent his eyes rounding. 'Good Lord, no! What did you think I was talking about?'

'I'm not sure. What were you talking about?'

'I only meant that I was going to be so damned impossibly good to you in every way that you would not be able to bear to leave me.'

Her heart flipped right over at his impassioned words, and she looked at her plate. Dear God, but she was in trouble here. Deep, deep trouble.

If she didn't watch it, she would end up doing what he wanted. Blindly. Mindlessly.

She could see herself not selling this house, not leaving Norfolk Island at the end of the month. She might even give up her career and her life in Sydney to stay here with him. Yet she knew in her heart it wouldn't work. It couldn't. He didn't love her. Besides, she didn't want to live here. Not forever.

'Say something, Jess,' he said, and she looked at him.

'What would you like me to say?'

'Tell me you want me as much as I want you.'

'You know I do,' she whispered huskily.

'You wouldn't lie, would you?'

'No.'

He smiled then, a smile that stirred her heart as no man's smile had ever done before.

Jessica knew then. Her feelings for Sebastian were no longer just lust. She was in love with him.

Oh, no…

She dropped her eyes and went back to eating her meal.

CHAPTER THIRTEEN

'YOU were right,' she said, looking up with a sigh from the shoe box. 'There's nothing. Not a mention of my mother. Not even an old photograph of her.'

Jessica was sitting cross-legged on Sebastian's bed while he was at his desk. He'd been writing while she sorted through everything.

He swivelled in his chair to face her. 'I did try to tell you, Jess,' he said gently. 'But seeing is believing.'

Jessica frowned. 'She must have burnt a lot of things. There's not much here. The only things I would want to even keep are these photographs of my grandparents, and Aunt Lucy as a child. Oh, and I suppose I can't throw out the one of her wedding. I must say that husband of hers was a very good-looking man. He could have been a movie star. I can see why she was besotted with him.'

'Handsome is as handsome does,' Sebastian said brusquely. 'He was a bastard.'

'I'm not saying he wasn't. I'm simply saying he was a looker. Tell me, Sebastian, do you know anything at all about his background or family?'

'No. Neither did Lucy, from what I can gather. He jumped ship onto the island when he was a young man, got a job on a fishing boat and married Lucy within a few short months. I might be cynical, but in view of what Lucy found out about him just before she died, I dare say he married her to ensure he could never be tossed off the island, not because he loved her. It's the surest and quickest way of making one's stay here permanent, by marrying an islander. You *can* earn permanent status by buying a business and working it for five years, but a man like Bill Hardcourt liked things quick and easy, I reckon.'

'Who was it that told Aunt Lucy about her husband being unfaithful?' Jessica asked.

'The doctor who diagnosed her cancer. Apparently, he'd known Lucy for eons. They were having a long heart-to-heart when he blurted that he'd always felt guilty about Lucy believing she was sterile, when he suspected her husband had had a vasectomy. It seems that shortly after Bill had been killed, the doc heard that Bill had been drinking heavily one night some years before and boasted that he'd had himself fixed up so he could tomcat around without consequences. He muttered something about having knocked up one girl too many.

'The doc remembered that round the time Lucy was engaged to Bill, he had a young girl patient who refused to name the father of her unborn baby because he was an engaged man and she didn't want to cause any trouble. She subsequently went to the mainland to have an abortion and never returned. Since Bill was dead by the time the doc worked all this out, he never said anything to Lucy. But it had played on his mind ever since.'

Sebastian scowled with displeasure at the story he'd just related. 'Personally, I think the old fool should have kept his stupid mouth shut. He eased *his* conscience whilst destroying Lucy's peace of mind.'

Jessica agreed with him. 'You're right, Sebastian. He shouldn't have told her. It must have been soul-destroying for Aunt Lucy, finding out the man she'd loved all these years was nothing but a low-down rat, and a filthy liar, to boot.'

'There again,' Sebastian sighed, 'I think down deep Lucy might have suspected the truth, but refused to believe it till confronted with evidence from someone she trusted and had faith in.'

'Yes, she must have heard rumours about her husband, living in a small community like this.'

'Evie said everyone knew about Bill's womanising. It's even said that he didn't fall overboard by accident, either. The man who owned the fishing boat had a pretty young wife.'

'Serve him right!'

'I couldn't agree more,' Sebastian said tersely. 'There's nothing worse than unfaithful husbands. And wives,' he added bitterly.

Jessica wasn't really listening to him, her thoughts on another tangent. Suddenly, her head jerked up, excitement coursing through her. 'That's it, Sebastian! That's it!'

'What's it?'

'That young girl. The one who became pregnant just before Lucy married that creep. I'll bet my mother found out about it and told Lucy, only Lucy wouldn't believe her. No doubt Bill made up a pack of lies to defend himself. He probably called my mother a troublemaker and a liar. Maybe he even made Lucy choose between him and his sister.'

Jessica was bouncing up and down on the bed with excitement at finding a logical solution to the puzzle. 'Well, what do you think?' she asked eagerly. 'Do you think I could be right?'

Sebastian was irritatingly unenthusiastic. 'You could be, I suppose.'

'You think I'm being melodramatic, don't you?'

'Lord, no,' he said dryly. 'I'm sure another woman could have come up with a much more torrid story.'

Jessica sighed with satisfaction. 'Oh, I feel so much better now. I just *know* that's how it happened. Evie told me she saw my mother and that disgusting Bill person arguing on the side of the road one day. My mother even pushed him over. That was very brave of her to do that, wasn't it? He was a big man.'

'Very brave.'

'What a shame Lucy didn't believe her.'

'It's difficult to believe badly of someone you genuinely love and trust.'

'I suppose so,' she said thoughtfully, before flashing Sebastian a speculative look. 'You're not trying to tell me something, are you? You're not a serial killer, or an international jewel thief, or an embezzler?'

'Not quite.'

'But there's something, isn't there? What haven't you told me, Sebastian?'

'Where would you like me to start?' he said ruefully.

'Wherever you'd like to start. I want to know everything about you.'

'Everything?'

'Yes, everything.'

His eyes went a cold steely blue. 'In that case, I suppose you'll want to know about my marriage.'

Jessica gaped at him. In all this time, this was one thing that had never occurred to her. Sebastian married! Oh, God, this was much worse than his perhaps having slept with Aunt Lucy. Much, much worse!

'Plus my divorce,' he added, and she almost burst into tears with relief.

But then another thought struck and she groaned.

'Don't tell me you've got children!'

He laughed. But it was not a happy sound. 'I thank God every day that Sandra refused to have any. She was waiting, supposedly, for me to make us both financially secure before she took such a big step as ruining her figure for a family.'

Suddenly, Jessica saw his very real pain and was moved by it. Her heart went out to him, and she wanted to touch him and comfort him. She put aside the shoe box and climbed from the bed, coming over to settle in his lap and wind her arms around his neck. 'She hurt you a lot, didn't she?' she said with soft sympathy.

'You could say that.'

'Was she very beautiful?'

'On the surface. It blinded me to her very ugly soul.'

'What did she do, Sebastian? Tell me.'

'I don't like talking about it.'

'But you must.'

He sighed and hugged her close. 'Yes, you're right. I must. Lucy always said she would not be erased properly from my mind till I talked her out of my system.'

'Did you talk to Lucy about her?'

'Not in great detail. She knew I'd been married at one time. And that it ended unhappily. That's all.'

Jessica couldn't help being pleased that Sebastian had left this confidence for her and her alone. 'Was your wife unfaithful?' she asked gently.

'Continuously.'

Jessica could hardly believe it. If she were married to Sebastian she would never ever even *look* at another man. 'But why didn't you leave her? Why did you put up with it?'

'Because I had no idea at the time. You know the adage. Love is blind. I only found out when she made the mistake of picking up someone who worked in the bank I was employed in. She'd met him in a bar and given him a false name to cover her tracks. She had no idea, of course, that this Casanova had a hidden video camera in his apartment. He brought some still shots in to work and was passing them round to his mates. When a close colleague of mine recognised the naked brunette who was being imaginatively serviced on a coffee table, he had the decency to take me quietly aside and tell me the situation. I was very grateful to him.'

'Oh, Sebastian, how appalling for you! What did you do?' Jessica asked.

'What did I do? I changed jobs and divorced my wife.'

'You're not telling the full story. Give me all the gruesome details.'

'Okay, so I punched Casanova's lights out, got fired, went home, packed my things, took a taxi to the advertising agency where Sandra worked, shoved the incriminating photo in her beautiful face and asked her why.'

Jessica wanted to know why, too.

'And do you know what she said?' Sebastian asked scornfully. 'She claimed it was all *my* fault, that I'd neglected her. She'd been bored, staying home so many evenings by herself while I worked late. Might I mention I was only working so bloody hard to give her everything she wanted. Sandra liked the good things in life. When I caustically asked her how long she'd been bored, she confessed since about a year after we were married.

'She assured me she hadn't been having affairs, only one-night stands. She imagined for some reason that that made a difference. She actually told me she still loved me.'

Jessica could not begin to appreciate the shock or the hurt Sebastian had suffered.

'That night I moved to Sydney, took the first of several medical tests, got myself a better job, worked my butt off, made pots of money, then, after a year of clear tests, started seducing every woman who so much as smiled at me. Believe me when I tell you it didn't take much to get them into bed.'

She believed him.

'What happened to all the money you made?'

'What?' he snapped, his body still tense with remembered distress.

'How come you lost your fortune?'

'I don't want to talk about money, Jess.'

'All right, then why did you decide to come to Norfolk Island?'

'I woke up one day and didn't like what I saw in the mirror.'

'What did you see?'

'A burnt-out wreck of a man who hated himself and everything around him. It felt like the air was crowding in on me, suffocating me. I had to get away somewhere I could breathe. So I drove to the airport and took the first small island destination that had a spare seat. The plane came here. I was a lucky man.'

'You're certainly not a burnt-out wreck any more, either,' she soothed, cupping his face and pressing feather-light kisses on each temple, his forehead, his eyelids. She drew back, and his eyelids fluttered open.

'What?' he asked, instinctively knowing there was something she wanted to ask him.

'I must know, Sebastian. Don't be angry with me. Did you sleep with my Aunt Lucy?' And she held her breath.

'Never,' he said firmly, and all the breath raced from her lungs. 'I told you...our relationship was a platonic one. I hadn't slept with a woman since I came to this island, till you came along.'

Jessica could hardly believe how wonderful that news made her feel. She'd thought she'd come to terms with his having slept with her aunt. But now she knew she hadn't. Not for a moment.

He cupped her face firmly between his hands and looked deep into her eyes. 'I love you, Jess. Surely you must know that by now.'

She found she could not speak, so great was her joy, so full her heart.

'I fell in love with you at first sight,' he went on thickly. 'I was furious with myself, of course. And with you. Because I feared you were another Sandra. By the time I realised my mistake I'd alienated you entirely. You've no idea how I felt that night when you took me up on my totally desperate offer. I made up my mind then and there that I was going to make love to you as no man had ever made love to you before. I thought, I'll *show* her how much I love her. I'll win her with the power of my desire, blind her with passion, seduce her with sex.'

'And you did, my darling. You did. I'm hopelessly, blindly, madly in love with you.'

She started kissing him all over his face, gently at first and then more passionately. When she finally kissed him on the mouth, he grabbed her and kissed her with a hunger that was as explosive as it was needy. He rose and carried her to the bed, drawing her down with him and making love to her with a savagery both primitive and satisfyingly simple. She held him for a long time afterwards, held him and stroked him and loved him till he fell asleep in her arms.

CHAPTER FOURTEEN

'ARE you going to do some writing this afternoon?' Jessica asked Sebastian as they washed up after lunch the following day. She'd spent most of the morning trying to clean the house while Sebastian made a total nuisance of himself, touching her all the time. And kissing her. And finally seducing her on the dining-room table. She'd just managed to drag her shorts on before Evie had arrived to make lunch.

He sighed with disgruntlement over the idea. 'I suppose I'd better. Do you mind?'

'Not at all. I've got some gardening to do.'

His eyebrows arched and she smiled. 'Yes, Mr. Smartypants, I discovered the other day that I do enjoy gardening. Now say I told you so and get it over with.'

He grinned. 'I told you so.'

'Don't get cocky. This still doesn't mean I'm not going to sell this place at the end of the month.'

His smile was distinctly smug. 'Wanna bet on that?'

Jessica laughed as she wiped her hands on the tea towel Sebastian was holding, then went outside to start weeding the garden beds. If she wasn't going to sell the place—and it seemed a likely possibility at this stage—she might as well keep it looking shipshape. Not that she was going to tell *him* that. Yet.

She was kneeling on the grass, about to attack the bed

near the front steps, when long brown legs suddenly appeared beside her.

'Hello,' the owner of the legs said when Jessica stood up, weeding fork in hand. 'You must be Lucy's long-lost niece. I'm Myra. I used to do the laundry for Lucy when she was running the place as a guesthouse. I was wondering, since you've hired Evie back to do the cooking, if you might want me to do your washing and ironing while you're here.'

Jessica looked Myra up and down with interest, her thoughts turning automatically to Sebastian.

The girl was about nineteen, very attractive, with a sultry mouth, a shapely figure and long straight honey-brown hair. A temptation, Jessica conceded, for any man, let alone a supposedly celibate one.

'I'm sorry,' she began, trying to be polite despite that automatic niggle of jealousy and suspicion. 'But I don't have that much washing and ironing. Not enough to hire someone.'

'But it's not just you, is it?' Myra countered, that sultry mouth turning slightly sulky. 'Sebastian's still living here, isn't he?'

'Yes, but he looks after himself pretty well.'

'Really? He never did when Lucy was alive. She waited on him hand and foot. Not that it did her any good,' the girl said, sneering. 'A man like that wasn't going to marry an old bird like her, no matter how much money she had. If Sebastian marries anyone on Norfolk Island,' she added, tossing her hair over her shoulder, 'it'll be someone young and pretty.'

Jessica found herself on the end of a sharp look.

'You're not staying long, are you?' Myra said. 'Word is you're going to sell and go back to Sydney.'

'I might,' Jessica said slowly. 'And I might not.'

The girl's eyes narrowed. They were not her best feature, her eyes, and narrowed, they looked sly. 'Is Sebastian in? I'd like to speak to him.'

'He's busy writing,' Jessica said firmly, 'and doesn't like to be disturbed. Can I give him a message perhaps?'

'He still writing that silly book of his? I thought he'd stop that once Lucy passed on. I reckon he only did it because it got him in good with her. He did lots of things to get in good with her, from what I could see. Not that it worked. She didn't leave him anything in her will, did she? Looks like he might have to get himself a real job now. Either that, or latch onto another rich woman quick smart.'

'I think you'd better go, don't you, Myra?' Jessica said coldly. 'You know, it's not a good idea to go around maligning people. You might find yourself in trouble one day.'

'I'm not maligning anyone,' the girl denied with a childish pout. 'I'm just saying it as it is. I suppose Sebastian claims he *wasn't* sleeping with your aunt. But he was. I know that for a fact. I'd watch yourself around him if I were you. You're much better-looking than your aunt.'

'I'll have you know,' Jessica said icily while trying to keep her temper, 'that Sebastian was *not* sleeping with my aunt, and if I hear you've spread this malicious gossip around the island, I am going to sue you for slander!'

'I don't need to spread what is already common knowledge. Everyone knows what went on here. If you're fool enough to be taken in by Sebastian's lies, then you're a bigger mug than your aunt. Just remember what I said when he professes love and asks you to marry him. It wouldn't be the first time a mainlander married an islander for reasons other than love.'

A few days ago, Jessica might have believed the girl's accusations, but now that she knew the man, she thought them quite ridiculous.

'If all Sebastian wanted was a marriage certificate to an islander, he'd have no trouble with silly little girls like you around,' Jessica pointed out crossly. 'Now go away and stop being a mischief-maker. I have better things to do than listen to jealous gossip.'

The girl huffed and puffed for a few seconds, then whirled on her bare feet and stalked off, her long hair blowing angrily behind her.

Jessica was standing there, staring after her disappearing figure, when Sebastian walked down the front steps.

'What did Myra want?' he asked.

'Her old job back,' Jessica told him.

He slanted her a horrified look. 'You didn't hire her, did you?'

'No.'

'Thank God. She's sex-mad,' he said. 'She made it perfectly obvious I could have her any time I wanted. No matter how rude I was to her she just didn't get the message. I was glad when Lucy closed the guesthouse after Christmas and Evie could get rid of her.'

'She said some pretty nice things about you, too.'

Sebastian laughed. 'I can imagine. Nothing worse than a woman scorned.'

'She suggested you might be out to marry me for reasons other than true love.'

'Did she now? And did you believe her?'

'No.'

'Why not?'

'Because it wasn't you.'

'Wasn't me,' he repeated, shaking his head in amusement.

'I figured if you'd wanted to marry an islander to wangle permanent status, or for tax reasons, you'd have done so by now. Myra would have been more than willing. Besides, you haven't asked me to marry you. Yet.'

'Do you want me to?'

'No. There is one thing I'd like to ask you, however,' Jessica added.

'Only one?' he mocked.

'Don't be facetious. I want to know how come you had such a supply of condoms on hand, if you were leading a celibate life?'

A decidedly guilty colour slashed across his cheekbones, and Jessica's stomach lurched. It seemed her faith in Sebastian wasn't quite total, after all. Or maybe the appearance of that sexy little woman had aroused more jealousy and suspicion than she'd realised. Myra *was* very attractive. And she'd been so sure Sebastian had been sleeping with Aunt Lucy.

'I bought them,' he confessed abruptly.

'But why? And when?'

'The day I took you to the chemist for your nail polish. Remember I bought myself a new hairbrush? Well, I picked up a couple of packets then.'

'A couple of packets,' she repeated numbly, aware that most packets contained a dozen. 'You bought two dozen condoms way back then, when you thought I hated you, and vice versa?'

'You can't blame a guy for hoping. Or for being prepared.'

Jessica's heart was thudding loudly in her chest. She wasn't sure if she was angry, suspicious or simply disbelieving. 'You were planning on seducing me even then?'

'Look, I had to do something, Jess! I was mad about

you, and so damned mad at myself for getting you off-side. I decided that afternoon to change my tactics some-what.'

'And you assumed I'd just come across?'

'I didn't assume, Jess. But I was hopeful.' He smiled a very sexy smile at her. 'I do have a pretty good strike rate with women...once I set my mind on one.'

She didn't know whether to feel admiration or exasperation. 'You're an arrogant bastard, do you know that?'

'I try not to be,' he said, and, drawing her forcefully into his arms, he kissed her till she was melting against him in glorious submission. 'How about coming to bed and making mad passionate love to me for a while,' he suggested, 'and then reading my manuscript for me? As much as I've done, that is.'

'You'd let me?'

'Of course! My body is always at your complete disposal.'

'Don't be silly.' She thumped him playfully on the chest. 'That's not what I meant, and you know it. I mean about reading your manuscript.'

'I'm having trouble with the ending,' he admitted. 'I want you to read what I've written, then I'll tell you what I was going to do and you tell me what you think.'

'Reading what you've written could take hours.'

'Why do you think I suggested bed first?' He scooped her into his arms and carried her inside.

'You're a devious man.'

'And you're a wonderful woman.'

'That kind of flattery will get you nowhere.'

'You're also beautiful, clever and incredibly sexy.'

'Ah, now you're talking...'

'Enough talking,' he muttered, as he dumped her on his bed and began peeling off her shorts. 'The only sounds I want to hear from you for the next hour are mmm, and aah, and ooh.'

Late that afternoon, after they'd made love leisurely for hours and abandoned any idea of Jessica reading his manuscript that day, Sebastian took Jessica swimming in Emily Bay.

It was a milestone in her life.

For she loved it. Loved the isolation. Loved the warm, quiet waters. Loved the peace that flowed through her body as she floated, feeling nothing but the sweetest pleasure over the knowledge that no matter where she was, if Sebastian was with her, she'd never be lonely again.

He took her with him to the pontoon in the middle of the bay, where they lay together and kissed and touched, oblivious of everything but each other. The urgency to make love again quickly overtook them, and he pulled her into the water with him.

Stripping her in the water was not easy, especially since she was wearing a one-piece with straps. Sebastian's brief black trunks were much more easily disposed of. Once they were both naked, he seated her on a rung of the raft ladder and pushed deeply into her. Jessica wound her legs around his hips and her arms around his neck and was soon lost in pleasure.

An elderly man walking along the beach with his wife of fifty-five years nudged her and pointed to the entwined lovers in the distance. They smiled at each other, silently recalling their own passionate courtship. Then they kissed lightly and walked on.

Afterwards, an increasingly besotted Jessica insisted Sebastian drive her past the gaol and tell her its history again, the one she'd missed the first time around. She wanted to know so that she could do justice to reading his book. He wasn't prepared to just tell her, however. He wanted to show her, insisting she get out.

'But I'm still in my swimming costume!' she protested.

'Look around. There's no one to see. The place is deserted. It's beginning to get dark, as well.'

Which it was, the sun having set while they were in the water, making love. Jessica gave in gracefully and climbed out, tracing the steps of the convicts as Sebastian relayed their cruel and inhumane treatment at the hands of their gaolers.

Jessica was both moved and appalled by all the horrors that had transpired within those creepy old walls. She shuddered as she viewed the flogging wall and gallows gate, but was truly shocked when she saw how small the cells had been, cells in which up to three men had been incarcerated, unable to even stretch out properly in their rough hammocks.

'I can understand how this place could inspire you to write a book,' she told Sebastian after they finally climbed into the car. Great drama could come from human suffering, and there were all the ingredients down there in those ruins for a fantastic story.

'You still haven't told me about your plot, you know,' she reminded him. 'Or the characters.'

'I've decided not to. I'd rather you just read the manuscript.'

'Then you'd better get me home so that I can start.'

He stared at her, and she was moved by the look on his face. So full of love and happiness. 'What did I say?'

'You called it home, not Lucy's Place.'

A lump formed in Jessica's throat. 'So I did.'

'You won't sell it now, will you?' he asked with soft

insistence. 'You'll be staying here…on the island…with me.'

He bent to kiss her before she could answer. But her response told him all he needed to know.

'Is there something you'd like to tell me, lovie?' Evie asked Jessica the following day after lunch. Sebastian was in his room, trying to write, and Jessica was helping Evie clear, as had become her habit.

Jessica thought about playing dumb, then decided it was demeaning to Evie. The older woman was nobody's fool and would have to be deaf, dumb and blind not to notice what was going on.

'I suppose you mean about me and Sebastian becoming lovers.'

Evie nodded smugly. 'I suppose I do.'

'Do…do you think Aunt Lucy would be disappointed in me? Or annoyed?'

'Oh, no. She'd be pleased as punch.'

'Would she? I'm not so sure about that. I think Aunt Lucy was a bit in love with Sebastian herself.'

'Well, you're wrong there! She might have found him attractive, but what woman wouldn't? Sebastian's a sexy man. If I were twenty years younger I might have fluttered my eyelashes at him myself. No, Lucy only loved one man in her life, and that was Bill. But she certainly admired Sebastian and thought he had a lot of fine qualities. She'd be very pleased to see you married to him.'

'Why do you assume I'll marry him?'

Evie looked perplexed. 'You're in love with him, aren't you? Blind Freddie can see that. Call me old-fashioned, but the way I see it people in love usually get married, if there's no reason they shouldn't. Is there any reason you shouldn't, lovie? You got a boyfriend back in Sydney?'

'No...'

'Well, then. What's stopping you?'

'Yes, what's stopping you?' Sebastian asked her as soon as Evie left after lunch.

Jessica frowned at him till the penny dropped. Then she waggled her fingers. 'Eavesdroppers do not hear anything good of themselves.'

'I only heard that bit. I was on my way to the bathroom. Well? You are going to marry me, aren't you?'

'I don't want to talk about marriage for now, Sebastian. Call me careful, but I can't help it. I love you to death and I'm quite happy to come back and live here with you. But marriage is a very serious step, and I need more time.'

'What do you mean, come back? Why don't you just stay?'

'I have to go back to Sydney, at least for a while.'

'Why? You can quit your job over the phone.'

'I don't want to do that.'

'Why?'

'Because you never know when I might want it back again. Or another job just like it.'

'Don't you trust our relationship to last?'

'Don't you trust me to go back to Sydney, even for a little while?'

He pursed his lips and thought about that for a while. 'I suppose so.'

'Just as well.'

When he went to take her in his arms, she backed away. 'Oh, no, you don't. You get that body of yours back to your book for a few hours.'

He groaned. 'It's still not going well.'

'How can it, when you spend all your time finding other things to do?'

He pouted. 'I like doing those things better. Besides, I'm waiting for you to finish reading what I've written so I can hear your verdict.'

'I'll be finished by dinner tonight if you'll just leave me alone. Now get back to work!' she ordered, and pointed to the door.

'Spoilsport,' he muttered as he left. 'Slavedriver!' he called over his shoulder. 'You'd have made a good warden down in that gaol!'

CHAPTER FIFTEEN

JESSICA was sitting on the back veranda just over three weeks later and only two days before her departure when a guilty thought came to her. She hadn't written to any people she knew in Sydney since she'd been here, hadn't even sent a postcard!

She bit her bottom lip and remonstrated with herself for her thoughtlessness. It was as though since falling in love with Sebastian she'd forgotten everything outside of her life here.

She'd become a different person from the woman who'd stepped off that plane, there was no doubt about it. For one thing, she didn't lock her car any more! What's more, she could actually sit out on this back veranda for well over an hour doing absolutely nothing except enjoying the warm breezes, the beauty of the scenery and the general peace and quiet.

Yesterday, Sebastian had taken her down to the pier at Kingston, where they'd sat on a bench on a hilltop overlooking the bay for three solid hours, watching a ship being unloaded. It wasn't at all boring, as she'd once thought. It had been very interesting.

The Jessica of a month ago would have scorned such simple, supposedly boring pastimes. Slowly, she'd begun to appreciate she'd been frittering her life away in Sydney, doing things she didn't really enjoy doing just for the sake of keeping busy, a legacy perhaps from all those years of seeing her mother wasting her life. Or maybe it was because she used to be so terribly, terribly lonely.

She wasn't lonely any more. She was also beginning to understand what Sebastian saw in Norfolk Island and its laid-back lifestyle. She could not wait to finish up work in Sydney, put her flat on the market and get back here to live.

Sebastian still wasn't thrilled with her going to Sydney. But she'd remained firm, believing that a short separation would do them both good. Their relationship had been so sexually intense this past month, it was hard to see things clearly sometimes. Sebastian could do with some time alone, too, to finish his book, his deadline having been put back to the end of March.

But what a book it was going to be! She'd been more than impressed when she'd read it. As for his idea for the climax and ending of the book—it was exciting and satisfying, but demanded a sequel, she informed him excitedly.

Already Sebastian's imaginative mind was forming the first chapters of another book about his hero, the unforgettable Tristram Marlborough, a handsome English nobleman who'd been cruelly framed by his evil and envious younger brother, then deported to Australia where his intractability caused him to be sent on to the infamous gaol on Norfolk Island.

What befell Tristram there would make the readers' hair curl, but would also fascinate them as their hero was degraded and tortured, starved and flogged by his jealous and perverted gaolers.

Jessica had no doubt that readers would want to know what happened after Tristram sailed off to sea in a small stolen boat. The last pages would see him rescued during a storm by a passing trading ship captained by an infamous pirate. Tristram was to bargain with him to take him back to England in exchange for promised riches when he would regain his earldom. The captain agreed, and the stage was set for the sequel.

'I'm off,' Evie announced, startling Jessica out of her reverie. 'Daydreaming again, I see.'

Jessica smiled and settled once again into the comfortable cane chair. 'I was thinking about Sebastian's book.'

'Going to be a winner, is it?'

'I think so.'

'You sure love him a lot, don't you, lovie?'

'More than I can say.'

'He's a good man. Lucy would be thrilled.'

Jessica thought of her aunt much more fondly these days, without any resentment at all. She'd come to feel a type of bonding with the woman since doing her garden and living in her home. But she still had a niggling suspicion she didn't know the whole truth about what happened between her mother and her aunt.

And she never would.

'I wish I'd had a chance to know her personally,' Jessica said with a sigh. 'And look after her. Was she in much pain towards the end?'

'Terrible. The doctor used to give her morphine, but she claimed it made her lose her mind, and she didn't like that much. Still, there were times when she just had to have it.'

'Oh, I feel awful that I wasn't here to help.'

'That wasn't your fault, Jessica. Think how happy Lucy would be knowing you've decided not to sell. She wouldn't care about your not running Lucy's Place as a guesthouse as long as it stayed in the family and was looked after and loved. How long do you think it will be before you can come back?'

'I'm not exactly sure. No more than four weeks. Sebastian will stay and look after the place for me. But I'll be back, never fear.'

'I know you will. Must go. I have friends popping by shortly. See you tomorrow. Enjoy your dinner out with Sebastian tonight.'

It was their habit to go out to dinner a couple of times a week in one of the many restaurants around the island.

'I will. Bye, Evie. Thanks for the lovely lunch.'

'My pleasure.'

Talking to Evie about her imminent return to Sydney prompted another guilty thought. She hadn't rung work once during the last month, either. She could have at least called Mark to see how he was managing. It was very remiss of her.

Not that he would really care after he found out she was going to resign. He was a very ambitious young man and would make an excellent public relations manager. She would recommend him for the job and hope management could overcome their ridiculous bias against hiring a man for the job.

Perhaps she would give him a ring now, see how things had been going.

Jessica rose and made her way to the telephone in the living room, perched herself on the wide arm of the nearby sofa and dialled. Mark's answer was quick and crisp.

'Public relations. Mark Gosper speaking.'

'Mark, it's Jessica.'

'Jessica! Great to hear from you. Don't go telling me you won't be back on Monday. Things are hectic here. I *need* you.'

'You *need* me?' she repeated, laughing. 'That's a first. It's me who usually needs you.'

'I never knew how much work you did till you weren't here,' he groaned. 'I've missed you like mad.'

'Well, it's nice to be appreciated. And I've missed you, too. I haven't had anyone here to bring me my morning cup of coffee. I've had to get it myself.'

'Poor Jessica.'

'Oh, I wouldn't say that. My stay on Norfolk Island has been…interesting to say the least.' Jessica smiled at this huge understatement. But she'd never been one to tell her private life to people at work. Or anyone else, for that matter. Even Sebastian hadn't been able to coerce much from her as yet, though he'd tried several times.

'I'll bet you've been bored to death,' Mark stated confidently. 'I'll bet you can't wait to get back here and at it.'

'No, definitely not bored. Not at all! But I won't deny I'm keen to get back. Though I don't…'

At a sound behind her, Jessica turned her head. The sight of a stony-faced Sebastian glaring at her from the doorway confused, then worried her. Had he overheard her conversation with Mark and misunderstood it?

'Jessica, are you still there?' Mark called down the line. 'Hello! Hello!'

Still frowning, she returned her attention to the telephone. 'I'm still here, but I must go, Mark. Sorry to cut you off like this. I'll see you Monday, okay?' She hung up and stood to face a still glowering Sebastian.

'That was Mark,' she said. 'My secretary. I thought I'd better give him a call.'

'A male secretary?' he drawled in caustic tones. 'How modern of you.'

'Don't go imagining things, Sebastian.' She tried a

sweet smile as she walked towards him. 'You *do* have a vivid imagination, darling heart.'

'Don't try to con me, Jessica,' he snapped. 'I know what I heard. The one thing I didn't hear, however, was your telling him you were quitting.'

Dismay held Jessica silent for a few seconds. My God, but he was quick to condemn. Maybe her one-sided conversation with Mark could have been misinterpreted, but he wasn't even giving her a chance to explain.

She couldn't help remembering the day Myra had come, making all sorts of nasty accusations about Sebastian. But she hadn't believed them, not for a moment. Because she felt she knew Sebastian, knew the man he was, what he could do and what he couldn't do.

One thing he *could* do, she realised unhappily, was be blindly, blackly jealous. He'd told her once a relationship was based on trust. Where was his trust, then? Was it so thin that one slightly ambiguous conversation could blow it away?

'Are you sleeping with your secretary?' he demanded before she could explain or voice her concerns.

'No,' she denied, trying to stay calm. But it wasn't easy.

'Perhaps I phrased that badly. I dare say one doesn't *sleep* with one's secretary. Are you *screwing* your secretary, Jessica darling? Does he bring you your coffee in bed in the mornings, or just at your desk, afterwards?' he asked, sneering.

'You've got a dirty mind, do you know that?'

When Jessica went to brush past him, he grabbed her arm and twisted her quite cruelly. 'Don't play prude with me, sweetheart. I'm the man you've spent most of the last month in bed with, remember? You did a damned good job of pretending to be pretty inexperienced at first, but it was wise of you not to claim complete innocence. That way you could become amazingly accomplished at sex with a lot more speed than some simpering virgin. How about telling me the truth now, lover? Just how many men *have* there been before me? Or are you going to claim your darling Mark was only one of the lucky three?'

She tried to pull out of his hold but failed. 'You're hurting me!' she cried, her face twisting with pain as his fingers dug deep. 'Let me go!'

'I'll let you go, all right,' he snarled, releasing her with a savage twist so she staggered against the doorframe. 'Right back to where you came from.'

'And that's where I'll stay, too,' she flung back, rubbing the ache from her arm. 'There's no future with someone as warped and twisted as you are!'

'And there's no future with you, you lying, conniving, deceiving madam. You're your father's daughter, all right!'

The immediate grimace of pained regret on Sebastian's face betrayed more than his actual words.

'What...what do you mean?' she asked, her voice faltering. She grabbed his arm and shook it. 'Sebastian, what are you saying?'

'I'm not saying anything, damn it!'

'Yes, you are. You don't even know my father, and yet you said...you said... Oh, no,' she groaned. 'I don't believe it. Not my mother and Lucy's husband! That's too awful to be true. And it *can't* be true! My mother didn't have me till over a year after she left the island. Tell me it's not true!'

'I can't do that,' he groaned.

'But how? *How?*'

'He met up with her again on the mainland,' Sebastian

admitted tersely. 'I think it was your mother's pregnancy that finally convinced him to have a vasectomy, not that other unfortunate girl's.'

Jessica felt her heart was breaking, so tightly was it being squeezed within her chest. 'I don't believe you,' she choked out.

He grimaced. 'Do you honestly think I would make this up?'

'You…you said Aunt Lucy hadn't told you why my mother left the island. You *lied* to me.'

'No, I didn't. Not technically. Lucy didn't tell me. She used to rave on while under the influence of morphine. She had no idea she was talking out loud, or that anyone was listening. I eventually put two and two together and worked out what happened.'

'Well, go on!' Jessica raged when he fell silent. 'Tell me. I want to know it all, every last pathetic putrid detail!'

'No, you don't.'

'Tell me! No more lies, either. The whole truth and nothing but the truth!'

'Very well,' he said. 'Lucy's sister came to her just before the wedding and told her she was in love with Bill and he with her. She said they were sleeping with each other. Lucy didn't believe her and Bill denied it, called Joanne a jealous little troublemaker. Lucy said she never wanted to see her again and Joanne left, devastated by her sister's hatred and her lover's betrayal. But that wasn't the end of it. Bill often went to the mainland, apparently. He must have looked up your mother and talked her into having another affair with him.'

'Why must he?' Jessica wailed. 'Why must I be his child and not the daughter of the man my mother married?'

'Because you're the spitting image of Bill, damn it! You'd have seen the likeness if you'd been a male. You have his hair and his eyes and his mouth. Lucy knew it the moment she saw you. It so shocked her she ran away. Before that, she'd thought of you only as Joanne's daughter, not Bill's.'

Jessica could only stare at him, too appalled to speak. She didn't know who to feel sorriest for. Her mother, for being so weak as to love a man like that. Lucy, for being betrayed over and over again. Or herself, for being the offspring of so ghastly a man. She hadn't thought much of her supposed father, but her real one was even worse!

'Jessica...' Sebastian reached out as though to take her in his arms.

'Don't touch me!' she snapped, her nervous system in a very fragile state. 'Go away! I don't want to speak to you ever again. I don't want to *see* you ever again. You don't love me. You don't trust me. I dare say you never even liked me. You lied to me more times than I can count. For all I know, you probably *did* seduce my aunt, for the same rotten reasons you seduced me. For this house. Or money. Or tax reasons. Or all three! You're despicable, Sebastian Slade, and I hate you!'

She could not look him in the face, for of course she did not hate him. She loved him. But she didn't want to have anything to do with him ever again. He had hurt her terribly this day, and she would never forgive him.

'I'll be putting this place on the market before I leave,' she said, her eyes fixed on a spot on the far wall. 'I want you out of here today. Be damned with the will! And be damned with *you*!'

'Jessica, I...'

When her eyes flashed black fury at him, he closed his mouth again.

'Don't even *try* to talk your way out of this. You'd be wasting your breath. I've known men like you before. Now get out! I'm sick of the sight of you.'

He looked at her for a long moment with a stony face, then whirled and walked away.

For a split second, Jessica almost ran after him, but in the end, she ran to her room instead, threw herself down on the bed she had not spent one single night in since the first, and wept as she had never wept before. Her tears seared into her very soul, for she knew she would never love a man again as she had loved Sebastian. Never.

CHAPTER SIXTEEN

'BAD news?' Mark asked as Jessica put down the telephone.

'No,' she said. 'Just business. Now where were we?'

'We were discussing how best to entertain the group of American VIPs we have arriving next week. They're only going to be here three days. Darned hard to show them Sydney in three days.'

'I agree. But what they miss out on, they'll never know, as long as what they do see is memorable. Put down a harbour cruise on day one, dinner here in the hotel that night followed by whatever's on at the Capitol Theatre. We've still got plenty of seats for the show there, haven't we?'

'Not enough.'

'Pop off and see what you can rustle up at one of the other theatres, then come back. By then I'll have figured out what to do with them on days two and three.'

'Right, boss. You sure do make snap decisions. But I like it,' he grinned, and turned to leave.

Jessica watched him go, a very good-looking young man who was also gay. If only Sebastian had known *that* when he'd accused her of sleeping with her secretary, Jessica thought bitterly.

Her mind turned to the phone call she'd just taken. It had been the solicitor, informing her that the sale of

Lucy's Place had been finalised the day before, with contracts being exchanged.

Jessica found the news depressing in the extreme. But it was done now, and could not be undone.

The buyer had been a company called Futurecorp, who refused to divulge their plans for the property to the vendor, though the solicitor thought it would likely be developed into a larger resort.

In hindsight, Jessica wished she'd put a covenant on the sale not allowing the house to be torn down or changed. But she'd been so upset and emotional at the time she'd merely demanded it be sold as quickly as possible for the best reasonable offer.

The offer had been more than reasonable, as it turned out. It had been exceptional. Jessica had originally consoled herself with the thought that if she could not be happy, she could at least be rich. Now, she wondered what insanity had possessed her. She should have protected her aunt's home and her own heritage. She'd let Aunt Lucy and herself down, and she felt terrible.

Tears welled up in her eyes. She was just reaching for a tissue when the telephone rang.

'Jessica Rawlins,' she answered.

'Jessica, Michelle here, from the front desk. I'm afraid we have a problem with the gentleman who booked into the presidential suite this morning. He's just rung down and demanded to see the public relations manager. I'm sorry, but he hung up before I could find out what about.'

Jessica sighed. 'It's all right, Michelle. I'll go up and see him. What's his name?'

'Mr. Slade.'

Jessica's heart missed a beat. It was not such an uncommon name, she supposed, but it was still an awful coincidence. A part of her began to panic. 'Do you have a Christian name to go with the Slade part? Or an initial?'

'Sorry. He paid with a company credit card.'

Jessica sighed with relief. Sebastian would not have done that. Neither would he have been in the presidential suite. It was another Mr. Slade.

'All right, I'll pop straight up and sort out whatever the problem is.' No doubt some trivial little thing. These company executive types could be so arrogant and demanding, especially when they were spending their company's money.

Jessica gritted her teeth and rose reluctantly from her desk. Where once she'd relished the challenge of soothing the most difficult guests' ruffled feathers, now she found such daily tasks a grind. There was no pleasure or satisfaction in her job any more, or in her life in Sydney. What she had once loved, she now hated. The hustle and bustle, the noise, the pace, even the smell.

She longed for the salt-sea breezes that wafted over the back veranda at Lucy's Place in the afternoon. Longed for the rolling green hills, and the warm waters of Emily Bay. Longed for...

She dragged in a deep breath as she punched the lift button for the top floor of the hotel.

I must not think of him any more, she told herself. *If I do, I'll go mad!* The man was devious, and wicked, and a lying con man, prepared to use his undoubted sexual charms for material gain, not only with her but with Lucy before her! And she wasn't just guessing about that any more. She knew that for a fact.

She hadn't really believed he *had* slept with her aunt, not even when she'd accused him that awful day. She'd been upset and angry, and wasn't thinking straight. Afterwards, she'd worried for a while that she might have possibly jumped to the wrong conclusions about him again.

But she finally reasoned if he'd been so damned innocent and misjudged, then why had he left within the hour? Why hadn't he stayed and fought for her love and trust? Any lingering doubts she still had about him had been obliterated the following Sunday when Evie had driven her to the airport.

For one of the passengers waiting for a flight that day had been none other than Myra, off to find work in Brisbane.

When Evie had left momentarily to go the ladies, Jessica had not been able to resist asking Myra exactly *how* she'd known Sebastian was sleeping with Aunt Lucy. And Myra had told her with blunt candour how she used to get the house early in the morning to do the laundry and how she'd seen Sebastian one morning, tiptoeing from Lucy's bedroom out through the French doors onto the veranda, wearing next to nothing, then sneaking to his own room that way. And this had been ages ago, well before Lucy became ill, when there were still guests at Lucy's place.

Given the circumstances, Jessica could find no reason for Myra to lie. It was Sebastian who was the liar, she concluded with despairing finality, like most of the men she'd ever known.

The lift doors opened and Jessica emerged, squaring her shoulders as she made her way briskly along the lushly carpeted corridor. The personal valet attached to the presidential suite was just emerging when she arrived. 'What's the problem with Mr. Slade?' she asked, her curt tone reflecting her mood.

'Problem?' The efficient young man's forehead wrin-

kled with a puzzled frown. 'He said nothing to me about
a problem.'

'He probably wants me to fix up a squash partner for
him,' she said tartly, 'or some such similar emergency.
Don't you worry about it. If you could let him know I'm
here before you go, I'd appreciate it.'

The valet nodded and disappeared for a few short seconds before reappearing.

'He's in the sitting room, having a drink,' Jessica was
informed. 'He said to go right on in.'

Her first impression was of superbly suited shoulders
and perfectly groomed brown hair. And that was only
from the rear. Mr. Slade was standing at the plate-glass
window, his back to her, his body silhouetted in the afternoon sunshine. Sydney's city skyline lay behind him,
dominated by the Centrepoint Tower.

'How do you do, Mr. Slade,' she said crisply as she
walked across the spacious room. 'I'm Jessica Rawlins,
the public relations manager. How may I help you?'

He began to turn, the light catching gold streaks in his
light brown hair as he did so. Jessica stopped breathing
once his face came fully into view.

'Sebastian!' she gasped, shock coursing through her in
a shivery wave. What on earth was he doing here? And
why was he dressed like that? Surely he hadn't come
after her, hoping to get her back?

He said nothing at first, penetrating blue eyes raking
over her, perhaps taking in her pallor and her thinness.
She hadn't had much appetite since her return from
Norfolk seven weeks before.

'Hello, Jess,' he said at last.

'You…you've had your hair cut,' she blurted, thinking
he looked incredibly handsome and suave, in a sleek,
citified sort of way.

Yet she didn't like his new image. Or was it simply an old one? Had he reverted to the Sebastian prior to his stay in Norfolk Island? The ruthless and decadent dealer who made and lost fortunes for other people and played Don Juan with promiscuous aplomb.

Lord, but he looked incredibly cool and intimidating in that grey three-piece suit and with his hair totally under control, not at all like the casually relaxed Sebastian she had met and fallen in love with.

How ironic that when she'd first seen him on the veranda at Lucy's Place, she'd scorned the idea of his ever playing the part of a business executive. He didn't have to play the part. He *was* the part, for real.

She looked at him at felt…what? Distress, but still desire. Dear God, she still loved him, would always love him.

It was a bitter pill to swallow.

'What is it that you want, Sebastian?' she asked, her voice strained. 'Why did you trick me into coming up here?'

'I didn't trick you. I gave my name.'

'Half-truths again, Sebastian?' she asked scornfully. 'Slade is not an uncommon name. You didn't give your Christian name. How could I possibly know it was you?'

'You must have suspected when you saw my company name.'

'Why? I never knew where you worked before, and I don't know now!'

'I do not work for a company, Jess. I *own* a company. It's called Futurecorp. The name must be familiar to you after the call from your solicitor today.'

Her eyes rounded to saucers. '*You're* Futurecorp?'

'Yes.'

'But…for how long? I mean, when did you…? I mean…'

'I formed Futurecorp several years ago,' he finished for her in a matter-of-fact tone.

Jessica's confusion was growing. 'Are you saying you're rich? That you've always been rich?'

'Not always. But for some years, yes.'

'Then you didn't lose your fortune before going to Norfolk Island?'

'I did make some unwise property investments back then, but no, I did not lose my fortune. Perversely, those same investments have come good during my stay on Norfolk. Ironic, isn't it, that my neglect has made me a wealthier man?'

Jessica thought it very ironic. And even more confusing. He obviously hadn't wanted to marry her for money, then, though the tax reason was still a valid contender. But if so, then what was he doing here? Why wasn't he on Norfolk Island conning some other gullible female? A man of his looks and wealth wouldn't have any trouble finding a suitable candidate.

'Did Aunt Lucy know you were rich?' she asked, frowning as she tried to make sense of everything he was saying to her.

'Not for the first year,' he admitted. 'She assumed— as you did—that I was bankrupt. I have to admit I found it…refreshing to know I was liked for myself and not my money. I also liked being helped and advised and cosseted. It soothed my soul to feel worthy of being cared about. I confessed my financial status to her when it no longer made a difference in our relationship. Lucy wasn't even angry with me.'

Jessica still was, though. *Very* angry. And very rattled by these astonishing revelations. She paced across the

room, then round behind an armchair, gripping the back
while she glared at Sebastian.

'Well, she wouldn't be, would she? The woman was
probably besotted with all the sex you were giving her,
just like I was! And don't lie to me about that any more.
I know you were sleeping with her.'

'No, I wasn't, Jess,' he denied again. 'Look, I know
what Myra told you that day at the airport. Evie tackled
her about it after you'd left to get on your plane. She
saw you talking to her. Believe when I tell you, Jess, that
I didn't make love to Lucy. Ever. But I did sleep with
her one night. That I do admit.'

What was the damned difference? Make love…sleep
with… He was playing with words again!

'It was the day Lucy found out about her cancer and
her rat of a husband. She was terribly upset. She needed
to talk to someone. But there were guests in the house
and we went to her room to be alone. We stayed up late,
talking. She became very distressed at one stage and
started to cry. I went over to where she was sitting on
her bed, took her in my arms and just held her. She
begged me not to leave her, and I didn't. I lay down and
held her till she went to sleep. Then I fell asleep myself.
There was no sex. I swear it.'

She stared at him, knowing deep in her heart he was
telling her the truth. But she couldn't bring herself to say
she believed him.

'Why would I lie to you?' he asked in the pained silence. 'If I'd slept with Lucy I'd tell you. Frankly, I
would not have been ashamed of it if I had. She was a
lovely woman. But she didn't want that from me. She'd
only ever loved the one man in her life, and bastard
though he was, she remained faithful to his memory to
the day she died.'

'Then why did you keep *me* ignorant of your wealth?' she demanded, confusion and hurt making her voice sharp. 'Because you found it *refreshing* that I liked you for yourself? Or was it that you didn't trust me, as you've never trusted any woman?'

'I'm not going to try to whitewash my behaviour with you. I haven't come here for that.' He sipped his drink, a bleak bitterness clouding his eyes. When he looked at her again, his chin lifted and he squared his shoulders, the actions carrying a dignified nobility that moved Jessica despite everything. How could she possibly admire him after all he'd done?

'I did love you, Jess,' he said. 'But you're quite right. Down deep, I didn't trust you. Even I can see that now. The trouble was that I'd experienced too many examples in the past of the aphrodisiacal power of money. Amazing how many beautiful women drop their pants for rich men. Age and looks have nothing to do with it. That's just an added bonus for the ladies in question. My strike rate was second to none in the seduction game, as I combined the best of both worlds.'

Jessica listened to what he was saying with some understanding and a large measure of guilt, conceding she'd had similar cynical thoughts about the opposite sex and their response to money. How could she condemn him for keeping his wealth a secret when she'd planned to keep even a modest inheritance to herself for the very same reasons?

'What I failed to appreciate,' he went on, 'was that not all beautiful women are like that, or like my chronically unfaithful wife. Basically, I was still as warped and twisted as you said, Jess. I'd fooled myself into thinking that I'd changed, that I was capable of truly loving and trusting a woman again. And I was—while I lived in a cocoon, and while I kept you in there with me. But it only took one small test to crack open the thin veneer of my so-called recovery.'

Jessica could not stop staring at him and thinking how brave it was of him to come here and say all this. How many men could admit to being wrong or weak? Not that she thought of Sebastian as weak. Just wounded.

But wounds could heal eventually, couldn't they? Given the right treatment. All they needed was some tender loving care. What Lucy had started, she could finish!

Jessica saw then that her love, too, had cracked under its first real test. She should have hung in there, not cut and run. She should have had more faith in Sebastian's love for *her*.

And he did still love her. She could see it in his tense face and his strained shoulders, in his actions as well as his words. The realisation moved her unbearably. Tears stung her eyes, and she had to blink to control them.

'You really bought Lucy's Place?' She choked the words out.

'Yes.'

'Why?'

'For two reasons. The first was to keep faith with my promise to Lucy to make sure her home was always looked after. I could not see it fall into unscrupulous hands, could I?'

Jessica's heart contracted. 'I…I shouldn't have sold it. I regretted it afterwards. Today, when I realised what I'd done, I felt so rotten.'

'I thought you might. That's the other reason I bought it, and why I have gifted it over to you.' He drew some papers from his breast pocket and handed them to her. 'Lucy's Place is yours now, Jess, to do with as you will.'

Jessica's mouth dropped open. 'But…but you've already paid me an exorbitant amount of money for it!'

'Call it conscience money.'

She groaned as she saw what lay behind these touching and generous gestures. Not guilt, and not just an ordinary love, but a very great love!

Oh, yes, he had hurt her, but only during a burst of irrational jealousy, and not with coldly deliberate cruelty. His act in not telling her about her real father was not such an unforgivable thing, either, given her father's wicked reputation. He'd probably been trying to protect her.

Jessica had come to terms with her parentage over the past few weeks, especially after a phone call to her legal father revealed he'd found out shortly after her birth that he wasn't her real father. He'd confessed to her that her mother's sick obsession with her sister's husband had been at the core of everything she did.

Her marriage—it had been a mad attempt to make Bill jealous. Her divorce—she'd fantasised Bill would marry her then. And her breakdown after Bill was killed—she'd turned to drink once her reason for living no longer existed.

The truth had not been a pretty story, but there had been a strange comfort in knowing the indisputable facts. Jessica no longer thought about her real father. He wasn't worth thinking about.

As for her mother, she'd been a very weak and self-centred woman. But she'd suffered for her sins. Jessica would not judge her any longer, especially now that she understood the power of love and desire.

She looked at Sebastian and thought how much she loved him and how much she wanted him. But did he want her? Did he want to try again? She was afraid he

didn't. There was nothing in his bearing or his manner
to indicate this visit was an attempt at a reconciliation,
just a monetary reparation.

'I don't *want* your conscience money,' she cried brokenly.

'Then what *do* you want, Jess?' Sebastian asked just
as brokenly. 'Name it and I'll give it to you if I can. It's
the least I can do after the way I've treated you.'

Hesitantly, she came round from behind the chair, her
heart in her hands as she reached out to him. 'I...I want
you, Sebastian,' she croaked. 'Only you.'

He gave a choked cry and gathered her to him, hugging her so tightly she thought she might snap in two.

'Oh, Jess...Jess,' he rasped. 'Do you mean this? You
really want me back?'

'For ever and ever, my darling. Life without you has
been unbearable. And I do not blame you totally for what
happened. I overreacted to everything. I should have
stayed and explained. For one thing, Mark, my secretary,
is gay. And I should have told you more about myself
and my past life, and the men I became involved with.
If I'd done that you would have known me better, and
you'd never have believed so badly of me. I—'

'Stop!' Sebastian broke in. 'You don't have to explain.
Or take any of the blame. In my heart of hearts, I knew
all along you weren't promiscuous or cheap. That was a
madman talking. I'm not that madman any more, my
darling. I swear to you. I'm so sorry for the things I said
that day. Please forgive me.'

Her heart melted at his heartfelt apology. 'Of course,
I forgive you.'

He shook his head slowly, in awe of her forgiveness.
'I don't deserve you. Dear God, I was in despair after
you left, but never more so than when Evie looked at me

and said, "Oh Sebastian, what have you done? She loved you. She truly loved you." I knew then what I'd done. I'd driven the woman *I* loved away. The only woman I'd ever loved. You made what I felt for Sandra nothing but a shallow sickness. I wanted to cut out my tongue for the things I'd said. I wanted to die rather than go on. I almost did die.'

'Oh, Sebastian, don't say such things. I can't bear it.'

'It's true. I stood on the cliffs at Rocky Point and would have cast myself into the sea below if I hadn't remembered something Lucy said to me once. True love doesn't die, Sebastian, she'd said. It can't. It lives, despite everything. It goes on and on and on. It was then that I decided to wait a while, then give myself one last chance of winning you back. I came here expecting nothing, Jess, but hoping…always hoping…'

'I'm so glad you came, Sebastian,' she said, hugging him. 'So very, very glad.'

'I love you, Jess. I love you so much. And to think you are going to give me another chance. I can't express how that makes me feel. So humble. So grateful. So happy. Kiss me, my darling. Kiss me.'

She kissed him and all the pain of the last weeks melted away. The loneliness lifted, and joy seeped in.

'Marry me, Jess,' he proposed. 'Have my children. Live with me for the rest of our lives.'

'I will.'

'You will? You really will?'

'I really will. Only…'

'Only what?' he said, instant worry in his eyes. 'You're not still afraid I want to marry you for tax reasons, are you? Let me assure I don't need to marry you for that. I never did. I bought a half share in a fishing boat and tourist business shortly after I arrived on

Norfolk. I'll soon have my own permanent permit, if that's what's worrying you.'

'It's not that, Sebastian.'

'Then what is it?'

Jessica gave him a sheepish look. 'Could you, um, please grow your hair again?'

'You don't like my hair this way?'

'Let's just say I prefer it long. And much as I quite like that suit,' she went on, 'it'll have to go, as well. I mean, if we're going to live on Norfolk Island, then this stuffy attire will never do.'

'You're prepared to give up your job and live on Norfolk Island? You won't be bored? Look, I'm quite prepared to move to Sydney if that's what it takes to make you happy, Jess.'

Jessica smiled. 'Sydney's a nice place to visit, but I wouldn't want to live here.'

His eyes shone as he pulled her to him again. 'I'll wind up Futurecorp,' he said, his voice strong and steady. 'And we'll go back to Norfolk to live.'

When he went to kiss her again, Jessica pressed her fingers against his mouth. 'Hold it there. What do you mean, wind up Futurecorp? What kind of company is it?'

'A family trust. I started it up donkey's years ago to help out the folks. It holds all my investments, from which I can disperse money to family members each year. Mum and Dad have now passed on, unfortunately, but I've been giving my three older sisters money each year. They seem to have married chronically unemployed men. I thought I might set up individual trust funds for each of them so that they'd be permanently secure, though that will substantially reduce my net worth. Does that bother you at all?'

Jessica pursed her lips. 'Not really. I have plenty of

money of my own after some fool paid me twice what Lucy's Place is worth. Still, much as I admire your generosity to your sisters, Sebastian, you seem surprisingly untroubled at giving up most of your fortune. For one who was once poor, that is. Don't forget, I've been there and I know *I* wouldn't give away most of my money, no matter what I wanted to prove. Is there something I don't know about?'

'Could be.'

'Tell me, you devil, or I'll throttle you.'

'I dare say you might.' He laughed. 'Well, these are the facts, ma'am. Yesterday in New York, my American agent auctioned off my sequel on a synopsis only for four million dollars. Of course, the winning publisher *had* seen a finished copy of my book. And now Hollywood's entered the fray. I'm sorry, Jess, but I'm destined to remain a rich man no matter what I do.'

For all his dry amusement, Jessica could see a small wariness remained. She reached up to lay a tender hand against his cheek. 'I think I can manage to love you rich as well as poor, my darling,' she said softly. 'I already did, didn't I? And what is money, when all is said and done? It cannot change what is in my heart. I'll love you for better or worse, for richer or poorer, in sickness and in health till death do us part.'

He covered her hand with his and looked deep into her love-filled eyes. 'Lucy was so right, wasn't she? True love doesn't die. It goes on and on and on. Let's not wait long to get married, Jess. I want to start having babies with you as soon as possible.'

Jessica's heart turned right over. Babies. Her own babies, with Sebastian as their father. It was her dream coming true.

'I see no reason to wait for a piece of paper to cement

our love, my darling,' she murmured, and, taking his hand, led him toward the bedroom.

'You know, Sebastian,' she said to him as they lay in each other's arms afterwards, 'I think this was what Aunt Lucy wanted when she put that clause in her will, throwing us together. She wanted us to fall in love and get married and fill her house with babies.'

'I think you could be right, my darling. She was a romantic, your Aunt Lucy.'

'And she was right. We did fall in love. And we are going to get married and fill her house with babies.'

'We certainly are, my darling. It's just a matter of time.'

Their son Tristram was born nine months later to the day. Their daughter Lucy followed fifteen months later. In all, Mr. and Mrs. Sebastian Slade increased the population of Norfolk Island by five. Sebastian's books went on to be international best-sellers. The movies based on his books broke all box-office records. They became very, very rich but it never changed their lifestyle, which remained simple and satisfying. They gave a lot of money away.

Jessica never worked again. At an official job, that is. She was more than fully occupied, with her husband, her children, her home and her garden. Evie continued to cook for them on a casual basis, though she was more friend than employee. They named their second daughter after her.

On their tenth wedding anniversary Sebastian took Jessica around the world. She enjoyed the trip but she was more than happy to come home. She loved Norfolk

Island more than any place on earth, though not as much as she loved her husband. Home, she realised, was wherever he was. He was her love and her life. He knew it, and treasured her accordingly.

Back by popular demand are

DEBBIE MACOMBER's

Hard Luck, Alaska, is a town that needs women! And the O'Halloran brothers are just the fellows to fly them in.

Starting in March 2000 this beloved series returns in special 2-in-1 collector's editions:

MAIL-ORDER MARRIAGES, featuring
Brides for Brothers and *The Marriage Risk*
On sale March 2000

FAMILY MEN, featuring
Daddy's Little Helper and *Because of the Baby*
On sale July 2000

THE LAST TWO BACHELORS, featuring
Falling for Him and *Ending in Marriage*
On sale August 2000

Collect and enjoy each MIDNIGHT SONS story!

Available at your favorite retail outlet.